# War Wounds

## A Marshall Family Western - Book 1

by

Wyatt Cochrane

This book is a work of fiction. Names, characters, places and incidents are products of the author's imagination or are used fictitiously. Any resemblance to actual events or persons, living or dead, is entirely coincidental.

© Copyright 2016 — Wyatt Cochrane

All rights reserved. Other than brief quotes included for the purposes of reviews, no part of this book may be reproduced by any means without prior written consent of the author.

ISBN-13: 978-1-7903-08798

# DEDICATION

To my wife and my daughters – my hope and my
inspiration

# CONTENTS

1    Chapter 1    1

2    Chapter 2    11

3    Chapter 3    15

4    Chapter 4    31

5    Chapter 5    41

6    Chapter 6    60

7    Chapter 7    67

8    Chapter 8    71

9    Chapter 9    78

10   Chapter 10   84

11   Chapter 11   91

12   Chapter 12   96

13   Chapter 13   107

14   Chapter 14   116

     Afterward    126

# Chapter 1

Thorn Marshall forced a smile and strode into the saloon. "Time to call 'er a night boys," he said to his men nursing beers the far end of the plank and whiskey-barrel bar.

"Awe Thorn," Red, the taller of the two men said. "We ain't had our turn with the girl. Them cowboys drinking at the other end got here 'fore us."

"How many of them have gone?" Thorn asked.

Art, the other man, grinned. "Two. Second one's upstairs now. Jes' four to go and then it'll be our turn."

"I'll give you boys an hour."

Glee burst across Red's face. "We'll be ready boss."

An hour later, everything packed and ready, Thorn buckled the straps on his saddlebags. He didn't mind the men having a little fun. Towns would be few and far between after tonight. When he walked into the saloon, his men stood in the same spot. "All right boys, time's up," Thorn said.

"But boss, we ain't gone up yet."

"I gave you an hour."

The bartender, a giant of a man, walked over. "Drink?" he asked Thorn, holding out a whiskey bottle and a glass.

"No thanks."

"The boys will be done soon, then you fellas can have your turn."

"We can't wait," Thorn replied.

"How about a drink on the house?"

"Thanks, but no. Come on boys."

Red looked from the bartender to Art to Thorn. "It won't be a minute now. Please boss."

They all looked to the wide wooden stairway as a grinning young cowboy, scampered down, followed by a heavy, older saloon girl with thin blonde ringlets.

Another young cowboy blushed and giggled "I reckon I'm next."

"You gonna be able to get your pecker hard this time?" one of the other cowboys asked.

"I reckon I am," the young cowboy said, his face glowing even redder.

"Hold on sweetheart," the woman said. "Give a girl a chance to catch her breath. Bring me a drink Randolph."

The bartender waved her over. "These gentlemen are in a hurry," he said.

The girl squeezed Thorn's upper arm and fluttered her eyelids. "I like this young one. Just as soon as I'm done with that last boy, I'll be ready for you men."

Thorn pulled away and shook his head. "Half hour. No more!"

A half hour later Thorn was back, and his men still waited. "Come on. There's a whorehouse on the edge of town. My treat."

"Closed," Red said. "All the girls are sick."

The bartender moved from the other end of the bar. "Seems like they ain't ready to leave," he said, as he walked around the bar toward Thorn.

"They hired on to do a job!" Thorn said. "Come on boys."

Red and Art started for the door.

"Hold on men," the bartender said. "I'll buy you a drink while you wait. The only one needs to go is this young fellar right here." He grabbed Thorn by the back of the arm and squeezed hard as he pushed him toward the door.

Thorn jerked away. "I don't want any trouble."

"It's all right," Red said, turning to the bartender. "You don't wanna do that."

The bartender grabbed Thorn's wrist and forced his arm behind his back. "I tried to do it the nice way." The big man lifted on the arm until Thorn's feet left the floor, his bent elbow and shoulder carrying all his weight. Just this way, the bartender had helped many drunken cowboys from the saloon to the muddy street.

Art shook his head. "You don't wanna do that."

Red, his face full of concern, stepped toward to the bartender. "It's okay. We're all going."

Thorn twisted, first one way and then the other,

3

but the big man held on and lifted him even higher. Once high enough, Thorn jerked his head back, catching the big man's nose. Blood sprayed. At the same time, Thorn kicked his legs higher than his head, then slammed them forward and down to the floor, throwing the big man over his shoulder and onto a nearby table. Splintered wood scattered around the room as the big man hit the floor and lay on his back.

As he followed Red and Art from the saloon, Thorn turned and tossed a gold eagle toward the big man, laying dazed and bleeding on the floor. "For the table."

*****

After Thorn left them, his men sat on dirty beds in the small run-down hotel room they shared. "Thorn's too damn serious," Red said.

"Yes sir," Art replied, "but he sure 'nough handled that big galoot."

Red bent over and laughed until he coughed. "Didn't know what hit 'im. The ol' Colonel taught that boy well."

"Shoulda taught him a man's gotta have a woman 'for he goes on the trail."

"Shoulda. And shoulda taught him a man needs a drink on the trail. Bet he never even thought of that."

"Go to sleep."

"Yep."

Two hours later, the rhythmic sound of bed springs creaking and bed posts bouncing on the floor above woke Red. He shook his partner.

Art sputtered and opened his eyes. "What the hell?"

Red held a finger to his lips. "Shhhhh. We're gonna get whiskey for the trail."

"Go to sleep! Everything's closed. 'Sides we promised we'd stay put."

"He won't even know we left and I ain't goin' without a couple of bottles. Come on," Red said, slipping into his pants. "Leave your boots off, 'til we get outside."

A few minutes later, Red tried the back door of the saloon. "Damn it! Try that window." Art pressed his palms against the glass and pushed. The window moved. Red grabbed his knife and pried, first one side and then the other until there was a good-sized gap. He worked the window up with his fingers.

"Git in there and open the door."

"Why me?"

"You're smaller. I can't fit." Soon, the two men crept through the back of the saloon. Red scratched a match with his thumbnail as they tiptoed into the main hall and behind the bar. Red stretched up onto his toes, pulled three bottles of whiskey from the top shelf and passed them to Art.

"That's enough," Art said, almost too quiet to hear.

Giddy, Red struggled to hold his laughter. "One more."

"Who's up?" the barkeep shouted from the second-floor. "Eileen?"

Red grabbed one more bottle, and they rushed out the back-door.

*****

At five a.m., Thorn, long awake, jumped out of bed, slipped into his clothes, and picked up his saddle

5

bags. He opened the straps and checked the contents one last time. Montana was a long way off. He tiptoed into the hall and tapped on a door a few rooms down. No reply. He knocked louder. Nothing. He tried the knob and found it unlocked. He eased the door open. Gone! Five in the morning and gone! He should have known better than to trust them.

He pounded down the stairs and checked the dining room, knowing they wouldn't be there. He marched to the livery. No one there. The saloon was dark. Everything in town was closed. Only one place they could be. The sheriff's office was dark, so he cupped his hands around his eyes and pressed them against the window. Unable to see the cells, he trotted around back. He leaped up and grabbed the sill of one of the two barred windows and pulled himself up. There, he found Red and Art sprawled on the bunks. He grabbed a bar with one hand, reached through with the other and tapped on the glass. They didn't move. Dead drunk!

The sheriff pointed a shotgun out of a second-floor window. "Who's there? Get away!"

Thorn dropped to the ground, keeping his hands high. "Just looking for my men. I don't want trouble. I'll come around front."

"You'll do no such thing. You'll come back at eight when I'm open. You and your boys have cost me enough sleep tonight."

At eight ten they should have been a couple of hours on the trail. Instead, Thorn paced back and forth on the boardwalk, waiting for the sheriff to open for the day.

Once in the office, the sheriff told Thorn the men had been found at three in the morning, drunk and pounding on the door of the whorehouse.

"What will it take to get them released?" Thorn asked.

"Well," the sheriff said. "Just being drunk and pounding of the whore house door would a cost them a night here and a little fine, but breaking into the saloon and stealing whiskey's another matter. The boys said their boss, I assume that'd be you, would pay for the hooch. I suppose if you paid Randolph for the whiskey and got him to drop the charges, I'd let these jaspers out for a ten-dollar fine."

"Ten dollars!"

"Each! Otherwise these boys are in my care until the circuit judge comes around in a couple of weeks."

"I can't wait two weeks. I'll pay for whatever they stole or broke. I'll pay a fine, bail them out…"

"Sorry, young man, but those boys ain't going nowhere, unless Randolph drops the charges." "If not, what happens?" Thorn asked.

"Judge'll probably give 'em another couple of weeks and a fine. Maybe more." "For a few bottles of whiskey?"

"Top-shelf whiskey. And the judges does like his top-shelf."

"I can't wait two weeks."

"Well young man, you do have a problem." The sheriff smiled and scratched his chin, "but it ain't my problem. Now get the hell out of my jail. I got things to do."

A few minutes later, Thorn pushed open the door to the saloon. The blonde sat near the bar, nursing a cup of coffee. She looked up and smiled. "Well look who's here. Come for your turn?"

"No Ma'am, I was hoping I could talk to the

owner."

At that moment the bartender, sporting a swollen nose and two black eyes, entered from the back. "What the hell are you doing here?"

Thorn held up his hands. "I'm here to pay for the whiskey my men took."

"That was my best stuff, but, sure, you can pay. Forty dollars."

"Forty dollars?"

"Like I said, it was my best stuff."

Thorn pulled two double eagles from his pocket and set them on the bar. The bartender took them and tapped them on his palm. "Thank you. I'll just put these away." He reached behind the bar and came up with a double-barrel shotgun.

"I don't want any trouble," Thorn said. "I just want to get my men out of jail."

The bartender cocked both barrels. "Shoulda thought of that before you broke my nose. Now get the hell out of my bar!"

Thorn shuffled back to the hotel and payed for another night. He tossed his saddle bags into the corner and fell onto the bed. How could they do this to him? During the war, they'd been like older brothers, always teasing and laughing and helping him deal with the bad. The Colonel called Red and Art his 'privates for life' and he'd warned Thorn not to let his friends drag him down. When Thorn had found them, down and out, it seemed right to offer them the job. He hated to leave them, but if he was going to make Montana before the snows, he would have to find other men—men he could count on.

By nightfall, it felt as if he had spoken to every person in town. Any man not already engaged had gone away to work on the Northern Pacific Railroad. Two big herds had come through town in the last month and taken a few more boys. Even the young cowboys from the saloon had ridden out at first light, heading home to Oklahoma.

The day drawing to a close, Thorn stopped by the sheriff's office. "I brought the boys' war bags," he said. The sheriff pointed to a corner. "Can I see them?" The sheriff pointed to the doorway leading to the cell.

Red sat on a dirty cot, his face in his hands. As Thorn entered, he looked up and grinned. "I knew you'd get us out."

"Not this time boys. Looks like you're going to be here awhile."

"We'll git on the trail as soon as we're out," Art said.

"Be too late."

"Did you find other fellars to go with you?" Red asked.

"Tried everywhere, but there's no one."

"Whatcha gonna do?" Art asked.

"I guess I'll go back to riding shotgun."

"What about your cows?" Red asked.

"Sell them I guess."

"Awe Thorn. We let you down," Red said. "It's all my fault."

"No. It's mine," Thorn answered.

"You can't give up," Art said. "Out of all of us, you're the only one gonna make something of hisself. The ol' Colonel knew that. Hell, we all did."

"You just gotta keep going," Red said.

Sleepless hours later, Thorn tossed and turned. Maybe he could drive his little herd by himself. If he got as far as Ogallala, he would find cowboys to ride with him to Montana. If not Ogallala, surely Cheyenne.

After breakfast, he spotted a cavalry sergeant and two soldiers walking into the general store. He rushed over. "Sergeant, excuse me."

The sergeant turned. "What can I do for you son? Are you looking to enlist? You'll have to see our barber first," he said, with a big smile on his face.

"No ssssir. I don't want to enlist. I'm, I'm driving a little herd toward Ogallala or Cheyenne and I'm wondering if there' been any Indian trouble out that way."

"Matter of fact, we got back from Cheyenne yesterday and had a quiet trip."

"How was the grass and water?"

"Good, once you get off the beaten track. There's been a couple of herds and several wagon trains, so you'll have to skirt a little wide of the main trail. When are you leaving?"

"I'm thinking I'll leave today."

"Good luck son. It's been quiet, but tell your crew to keep their eyes open and their powder dry. Them Cheyenne and Arapaho would like that pretty blonde scalp like yours."

# Chapter 2

Thorn opened the gate to the corral holding his little herd. The late morning breeze blew cool. It was a good day for a cattle drive and a good day to be alive. After two days locked up eating dry prairie wool hay, the red, white-faced cattle were eager to get out on fresh grass. Thorn laughed as the twenty cows and the big bull all tried to push through the gate at the same time.

The cattle had caused quite a stir when he and his two jailbirds drove them into town. Out west, other than milk cows, people rarely saw anything other than the multi-colored herds of rangy longhorns that passed for beef. Thorn had purchased the Herefords from a Union captain he met during the war. He'd spent a good part of the money, the Colonel had left him, to buy the little herd. Most of the money came from the pain and suffering of others, but just like you can't put a head back on once you've lopped it off, you can't change the past, and he'd decided to do the best he could with the money.

The cattle bucked and jumped, enjoying the freedom. Thorn laughed. "Feels good to be on the trail, don't it?" He loved these Herefords. A herd of longhorns may have stampeded off, but the docile Herefords soon dropped their heads and grazed on the green shoots pushed up by recent rains. Once he had enough blood stock, he would cross the Herefords with longhorn cows and breed some wildness out and more beef in.

He was excited to get to Montana, where there was still free range, and build a ranch with his wits and his own two hands. After growing up in the middle of the war, he wanted to live in peace. He would sell beef to the men working on the railroad and, once they finished the rails, ship it on the cars to hungry folks back east.

Before starting the cattle, Thorn closed and latched the gate, found a pitch fork and cleaned up around the corral.

The old man looking after the stockyards wandered over and leaned on the fence. "Thanks for doin' that. Most don't."

"You're welcome."

"Where's your boys?"

"Jail."

"Jail?"

"Yep."

"Got more coming?"

"Nope."

"Usually takes at least three to move a herd."

"Yep."

The old man smiled and shook his head. "Good luck."

Thorn took up the lead rope of his pack horse and rode out to the grazing cattle. The buckskin felt strong between his knees. He whistled and whooped. His cattle raised their heads and started moving. The one-horned cow didn't want to leave the green grass and tried to cut around him. The buckskin saw her and cut left to turn her back. Thorn almost fell off when the pack horse failed to come along. He had to drop the lead rope to stay in the saddle. Now free, the pack horse trotted a short distance then dropped his head and grazed.

Thorn left him grazing and slowly worked the cattle into a tight group. Finally, he got them out of town and headed west. He could do this! By the time he rode back and caught the pack horse, the cattle had stopped and were grazing contentedly.

Whistling and hollering, he trotted back toward the herd. The cattle raised their heads but did not move on. He tried to drive them with the pack horse in tow. By the time he got the cattle on the left to move, those on the right stopped. By the time he led the pack horse to the right, the cows on the left had stopped. He tossed the lead rope over the pack horse's neck. He hoped that once the cattle were moving well, the herd instinct of the pack horse would kick in and he would follow the buckskin. Not so. The pack horse refused to follow, and every time

Thorn left the cattle to get him, the cattle stopped.

After more than an hour, his buckskin lathered and the cows grazing less than half a mile from town, reality sank in. What was he thinking? He had to find men. He turned back to catch the pack horse and take him to town, then he would return for the cattle. Even getting the cattle back to the corral would be difficult, if not impossible, without help.

I hate cows, he thought as he snatched up the lead rope. The pack horse bolted and galloped, kicking out and farting, around the herd to the top of a hill where he stopped—almost a quarter mile west, then dropped his head and grazed. "I hate horses too." Thorn slumped in the saddle, shaking his head. Even if he'd been able to get the cattle going, how would he have herded them all day and guarded them from Indians and predators all night. He'd been a fool.

He looked up and noticed the high-horned cow, that usually led the herd on the trail, moving toward the pack horse Three of the other cows and the bull followed her. He eased the buckskin up on the stragglers, clucking at them until they moved along toward the lead cow. Once he had pushed them a couple of hundred yards, the lead cow remembered the trail and lined out. The rest of the herd followed her. As they trailed by, Thorn caught the pack horse. He could do this! Ogallala was a cattle town. He would find men there and, if not, he would surely find help in Cheyenne.

As far as sleeping went, he was young, and like the Colonel had often reminded him: 'You can sleep when you're dead.'

# Chapter 3

Elly Strong choked back her fear, holding it tightly down, as she hugged the women of the wagon train and said her goodbyes. Tears welled, but she blinked them back. They hadn't planned to stay with the wagon train as far north as Scottsbluff, but the prairie fire had forced a change of plans. With nothing for their horses to graze on between Ogallala and Cheyenne, they had no choice but to skirt the blackened ground.

Now, after two months traveling the Oregon Trail with the wagon train, she didn't want to be alone in this vast land with her two supposed business partners. When Martha Morgan suggested that she come on to Oregon and offered her a spot in their wagon, Elly almost changed her plans. John, Martha and their son and daughter reminded her of her own family, before the war.

In the end she decided, that with less than a hundred miles from Scottsbluff to Cheyenne, she would push through to be with the only blood family she had left. Then she would be rid of these men forever, even if it meant giving up her share of the business. Her goodbyes said, the wagon packed, and the team hitched, she waited for the two men and pondered how she had come to be here.

\*\*\*\*\*

The grass had waved green and lush on that spring day, two months prior. With no one cutting it anymore, they brushed through, knocking it down with their shoes. The mound of dirt lay, red and accusing, against the green beyond the open grave. The wooden box, her mother's last bed, was gray and speckled, made from lumber salvaged from the Grand Hotel, where no one would ever stay again.

The singing and word saying done, Elly stepped up and placed a small bouquet of wild flowers over the spot, she imagined her mother's heart to be. She nodded, her cheeks dry, no tears left.

Four old men untied rough ropes from the stakes that held them and gently lowered the casket into the ground. The gray box came to rest on small mounds of dirt left in the bottom of the hole. This allowed the ropes to slide easily from beneath it. They knew how to bury in Breedlin, Missouri.

Elly walked around to the dirt pile, but instead of tossing in a handful, she picked up a shovel, plunged it into the red dirt, and threw shovelful after shovelful onto the casket—thump, thump, thump. The friends and town folk gathered at the graveside looked on, not sure what to do, until dear Mrs. Branscombe, picked up the other shovel and started filling the other end of the grave. As Mrs. Branscombe tired, one by one, the others took the shovel. Mr. Branscombe gently placed a hand on Elly's shoulder and reached for her shovel, but she shrugged him away and kept throwing dirt—whumpf, whumpf, whumpf.

Only when the shoveling was done, the red dirt mounded and tamped, and her friends and family shrugged away, leaving her all alone, did Elly allow herself to sink to her knees and remember another day, a few years earlier, near the same spot.

\*\*\*\*\*

That was the day Conrad Kehaler brought his best friend, her darling brother Gus, home. She was humming a little tune as she swept out the back room of her father's store.

"It's Connie!" her father said.

She ran to the front of the store, missing the fear in her father's voice. Thrills rushed up and down her spine as she hurried to see the dashing young soldier. A man now, but still the older boy she'd often imagined she'd one day marry.

When she saw Connie, no one had to tell her it was bad. His gray uniform, covered in mud and blood, and the borrowed buckboard, hitched to a team of foam-covered horses, told all.

*****

A few weeks earlier Gus and Connie, full of excitement, passion, and righteous anger, had left to serve. Neither family owned slaves, but both believed it was the right of the southern states to choose their own path.

"Take care of Gus for me Connie," Elly's mother had said, as the boys prepared to march off.

"I will, Mrs. Strong. I promise," Connie said. Elly's heart swelled, seeing his strength.

*****

A cold drizzle had cooled the hot tears on her cheeks as they lowered Gus into his muddy hole. That day the rough, hemp ropes reminded Elly of the swing behind the store—where Gus and Connie once pushed her so high, she had fallen and broken her arm.

"No," she cried, dropping to her knees as they lowered Gus down.

Her father knelt, put a loving arm around her shoulders, and held her close, but her mother, lost in her own grief, failed to notice the broken girl kneeling in the mud at her feet.

Now her mother forever rested between her husband and her son.

*****

Today, Elly Strong had to leave the past and

decide. Breedlin, Missouri was the only place she'd ever lived. Her mother, father, and brother were all buried here. She longed to stay, but the town was dying. In fact, it was all but dead, having never really recovered from the wounds inflicted the day her father was murdered.

She unfolded the heavily creased telegram and read it again. 'Sorry about your mother. Love home work for you here. Aunt C.' Her Aunt Caroline lived with her husband, Raymond and their new baby girl, Adeline, in the frontier boom town of Cheyenne, Wyoming.

Mrs. Branscombe glanced up as Elly entered the store. "Have you decided? You know, you're always welcome to stay with us, for as long as we can hold on."

Elly smiled. "I do want to stay." And she did want to—more than anything. "But I see how things are going, between the war and us not being on the rail line. I see you taking things, you can't sell, in trade for things, you need to sell." She held up the telegram and said, "It sounds like things are good in Cheyenne, and Aunt Caroline and her family are the only blood kin I have left..., but I hardly know them. And Cheyenne sounds like.... Well anyway, Breedlin's all I know."

"I don't know what we'd do without you. You've been like a daughter to us since we bought the store. You taught us most of what we know about running the place."

"Nonsense. I don't know how I could ever repay all that you two have done for me since Daddy died, what with the way Momma never really came back."

Mrs. Branscombe placed one hand on Elly's shoulder and raised her chin with the other. "Losing a son and watching your pa murdered, took all the starch out of her, but before the war she was a fine woman, with a big heart. I know you're grieving, but she's finally at peace and you've grown into a fine woman. Now you can find your own life."

Elly knew what she had to do. It hurt to think of giving up the one thing remaining to her that her father had cherished. His team was his pride and joy, his only extravagance. He had purchased the black Percheron geldings in Kansas City and anytime something troubled him, he brushed and groomed and whispered to the gentle giants.

"Do you think you'd want Daddy's freight wagon and the team?" Mr Branscombe, on the far side of the store, looked up from his sweeping. "If I could give you a fair price, I'd take them in a heartbeat, but I can't."

"I wish I could just give them to you. You need that team and wagon to haul freight for the store, but Momma had nothing left and all I have is a few greenbacks I've saved."

"Oh Elly, that's a kind thought," he said. "I didn't want to tell you before, but Mrs. Branscombe and I might have to let the store go and move. We're afraid there might not be enough left here to keep going."

Elly stepped close and hugged him. "I don't know how you've stayed this long. If I can sell the team and wagon, I'll buy a ticket and ride the train to Cheyenne."

*****

The next morning, Elly walked up to the livery stable. Old Mac perched on a three-legged stool, drank coffee with the two preacher men.

The preachers had drifted into town a few days prior, leading an old pack mule and selling themselves as itinerant men of God. They'd scrounged up planks and nailed together a few rickety benches in the big front room of the late Widow Andersen's abandoned house. Benches built, they stood outside and shouted for people to come and be saved. When no one came, the smaller man started singing. He had crooked tobacco-stained teeth, a pinched face, and a pointy rat-like nose, but he had a beautiful, booming singing voice.

What the shouting couldn't do, the singing did and, like rats to the Pied Piper, the people filed from their homes and into the makeshift church.

Her father had taught her to be cautious of traveling salesmen of all kinds, but starved for excitement and entertainment, Elly slipped into the back of the room.

The smaller man began by leading a hymn sing. As the newly formed congregation joined in, the hymns grew faster and louder, until the room buzzed with energy and excitement.

Elly, who had not so much as hummed a tune since her father's murder, found herself mouthing the words, then whispering and finally singing at the top of her lungs. She had loved singing and once she started, she didn't want to stop.

Eventually, the taller preacher moved to the makeshift pulpit and shouted: "Brothers and Sisters of Breedlin. As I look out at you singing and praising Jesus, I feel hope. We've suffered so much."

"Amen," someone in the crowd shouted.

"Amen brother. The war has taken so much from

us all," he preached.

"Amen! Amen!"

He continued to preach about the devastation and suffering brought on by the war. The more he preached, the louder the crowd grew.

"When I look out at you good people, I think of the old prophet Job. Now Job was a blessed man living in the Land of Uz, a land not unlike the town of Breedlin before the war. Job had flocks and sons and daughters and friends and everything a man could want. Then one day, the old Devil came to the Lord and said: 'Job only loves you because of all you gave him.'"

"And the Lord said: 'Not so.'"

"But the Devil wanted to prove the Good Lord wrong, so the Lord agreed to let him test Job. And Old Scratch had him a time. He took Job's sons and his daughters. He took his flocks and his lands and left Job naked and sore. Just like what's happened to you good folks here in Breedlin. Everyone about, thought Job must've done something awful, for God to punish him that way. But in the end Job proved them all wrong and Old Scratch had to slink away, his pointy tail 'tween his legs. Job took up what little he could find and gave it to the servants of the Lord, and God rewarded him for his faith, his generosity, and his gifts, and God returned to him more than he had before: more lands, more cattle, more sons, more daughters, and Job lived the rest of his life in a land of milk and honey."

"Amen!" the smaller preacher shouted.

"Amen! Amen! Hallelujah!" Elly chanted along with the others.

Suddenly the tall man held out his hands palms

down and quieted the crowd. Then he held his finger to his lips and silenced them. "Today, my brothers and sisters—the Lord Jesus sent me and brother Herb to bring you a message of hope. Today, the Lord Jesus will show you a sign. The Good Lord has not forsaken the people of Breedlin. Behold the miracle of the Lord."

He knelt and reached behind the makeshift pulpit. A rattly Tddddddd td td td filled the room. The tall preacher moved slowly…, slowly, then quickly. Next, he carefully presented a four-foot-long rattlesnake to the room. Holding it behind its diamond-shaped head he gently raised the writhing, rattling snake and then thrust it out to the end of his arm.

As one, the congregation jumped back.

The preacher stroked the beast with his free hand and before long it stopped rattling. He took it by its midsection and the snake firmed its back, balancing itself on his open hand. He walked through the crowd swaying and swinging, parting the congregation as he moved around the room, the snake leading the way.

He sped up; pranced back and forth across the front of the room, one hand in the air. He shouted praise. The crowd started shouting along with him. He thrust the snake into the air. "Amen!"

Elly raised her hands and answered with the rest of the crowd. "Amen!"

"Hallelujah!"

"Hallelujah!"

"Praise Jeeeeeeesuus!"

"Praise Jesuuuuuuuuuuuus!"

They shouted back and forth until Elly felt the room and her very heart might explode. She felt unbelievable hope. She could stay forever in this town, the only place she had ever lived, with these people, her lifelong friends and neighbors. She felt that God could restore hope and restore the town.

Mesmerized, Elly drifted around the side of the crowd to a spot off the front of the room. The man stopped in front of her and inched the snake closer and closer to her face.

The snake undulated and writhed in his hand, its black forked tongue flashing, tasting the air almost touching her cheek.

The tall preacher paused until everyone went silent, then he leaned toward them and whispered. "Fear not, saith the Lord. For I am with you and I shall protect you. Even from the serpent."

To Elly's surprise, even under the waves of energy coursing through her chest, she wasn't afraid. Arriving back at the front of the room, the tall preacher dropped the snake roughly to the floor. The snake coiled and restarted its warning rattle. Tddddddd td td td

The preacher stood straight, drew in a deep breath, and spoke, each word louder than the one before. "Fear not, gentle folks. The Good Lord said his followers will cast out devils and speak tongues and take up serpents and drink poison and THEY SHALL RECOVER!" He started an awkward stomping dance around the creature.

"Eyal Co Ho," he chanted in tongues. "Scallala Cola Ho… Eyala Hallala Co."

Soon Elly chanted along with the others: "Eyalla Co… Eyalla Co Ho. Eyalla Co… Eyalla Co Ho."

The tall man dropped to his knees right beside the snake and the snake struck him on the shoulder. The preacher's eyes opened wide and his face turned bright red. The snake hung for a moment then fell free and recoiled its body, its head weaving and swaying, prepared for another strike. Dots of blood stained the preacher's white shirt as he raised his hands skyward, then fell back. The room fell silent, and the people backed away, all eyes locked on the downed man.

As the tall preacher clutched his wounded shoulder and writhed in agony, the smaller preacher held his hands up. "The Good Lord will protect those who believe." Then he started singing. "Sing with me!" he shouted to the shocked congregation. "The Good Lord will protect!"

As the crowd sang, Elly's spotted the snake winding toward her, tongue flicking, eyes unblinking. Gently, as she had done as a child with corn snakes, she lay her hand in its path and, as it crawled over, she slowly, gently picked it up and caressed the dry, wax-like skin. Instead of the squeamishness she had felt holding corn snakes, powerful waves of ecstasy coursed through her.

The tall preacher's eyes fluttered open and the small preacher whispered, "Praise the Lord." Then louder, "Praise Jesus!"

"Praise Jesus," Elly whispered. "Amen."

The taller man trembled and swayed as he crawled to his knees. "Fear not good people," he whispered. "For like the great Apostle Paul, the Lord has spared me from the poison of the serpent." As he gathered strength, his whispers turned to shouts, and the congregation shouted back the words of praise.

As they shouted, the snake inched forward over Elly's hands. When it threatened to fall, she crossed her hands and gently drew it back to her. She felt the snake speed up and grow restless. She reached forward more quickly and kept the writhing creature close. She noticed a gunny sack draped over the side of the snake's box behind the pulpit. As she reached down to slide the snake in, the tall preacher fell silent, lowered his arms and watched, wide-eyed. As the snake disappeared into the sack, his eyes ran up and down her body. Bile rose in the back of her throat, the way it did when she had to pass by the men lounging on the porch of the saloon.

The spell broken, Elly looked around the dingy room. Instead of hope, she felt only sadness. The Breedlin she knew was gone. Forever gone. She gently folded the sack over the snake, slipped out of the makeshift church and ran home. As she ran, she cried for her lost town…, for her poor mother…, and her darling daddy and brother…, and she cried for herself.

*****

"Good morning Mac… Reverends," Elly said. She felt uncomfortable, awkward, talking to Mac with the preachers present. "I'd like to talk some business with you Mac. Could we speak alone?"

"Why I reckon it's the snake girl," the smaller preacher said. "We was jes talkin' 'bout you."

"Why it is," said the taller, tipping his hat. He looked pale and drawn.

Mac smiled and shook his head. "I heard you picked up that ol' rattler. You always was a bold child. What you got on your mind today, Elly dear?"

She hesitated, looked at the strangers and wished

them gone. "Well."

"Go on sweetheart," the tall preacher said. "Don't pay us any mind."

"Well... With Momma gone," Elly started, "I'm thinking of going to Cheyenne to be with my Aunt Caroline."

"Why that sounds like a fine idea, Elly. A fine idea, though we'd all miss you 'round here."

"Before I go, I'd like to sell my Daddy's team and freight wagon and I thought you might be interested."

"Me? Why that's a fine offer and a fine team, but I board horses. I don't need no freight wagon."

"I thought maybe you could buy it and hire Jeb or one of your other nephews to haul freight from the railroad for the store and for anyone else needing things moved. You could give me half what they're worth now and pay me the rest from you profits."

"Well now. You have been thinking. And that's a fine offer, but I'm too old to be starting a freight business and I guaranteed don't want to be going into no business with no nephew of mine."

The tall preacher raised his hands above his shoulders. "The Lord works in mysterious ways," he said. "My partner and I were just discussing a change of careers and we have a line on a load of freight that we could sell in the west. Perhaps we could come to an arrangement. The Reverend Wilford Adler's my name, but folks call me Wilf, and this is my melodious associate Brother Herbert Stump."

Elly experienced a rush of hope and then uncertainty. For while she needed the money to get to Cheyenne, for reasons she couldn't quite grasp, she didn't like the thought of her Daddy's beloved team going to these two men. Perhaps, though, the

Reverend was right. She had prayed for help selling the team. Maybe God did work in mysterious ways.

The tall preacher, Wilf, eased himself to his feet, his legs shaking. "Let's go have a look at them."

After a quick look at the black geldings and the wagon, Wilf said, "I think we're interested."

Elly was surprised at how little time and effort they had taken. She had watched her father buy many things over the years, always taking the time to scrutinize each item and to consider its value. She prepared herself for a low offer and asked, "How much would you give me?"

"Well, that is the problem," Wilf said. "We couldn't give you anything up front. The preaching business is not what it once was. Used to be a good sermon and hymn sing brought a week's pay. A man could live pretty easy on that alone, and if he were willing to endure the pain and suffering that comes with a snake bite, he could live like a king. Unfortunately, with the hard times today, saving souls is not the good life it once was."

The smaller preacher spoke up with pride in his voice. "Not many tough enough to take a snake bite the way Wilf can. Yet still…"

"Then what do you mean you're interested?"

The men told Elly they knew the trail from Breedlin to Cheyenne and offered to get her and her belongings there for the price of the team and wagon. When she hesitated, they offered her a quarter share in the freight business, though she would have to drum up freight business in Cheyenne as part of the deal.

"It could be profitable for all of us," the Reverend Wilf said.

"You could drum up business and we could get us a driver, and me and Wilf could manage things," Brother Herb added, brightening. "We'd be living in the land of milk and honey."

"Let me think on it," Elly said. "I'll give you an answer in the morning." Had she been able to get cash for the team, Elly would have packed her things and been on the train west in a week. Now she had to consider the possibility of spending two months or more in her wagon with these men she didn't know.

\*\*\*\*\*

Sitting on the dirt of her mother's grave, she pleaded–begged. "What should I do Daddy?" After hours of questions, but no reply, she stood, brushed the dirt from her dress, and walked until her legs quivered. Long after the sun had gone down, she decided. She would stay in Breedlin until she could find an outright buyer for the team. Quietly, so as not to disturb the Branscombes, she slipped up the back steps of the store to the small room she had shared with her mother. She slept fitfully.

After a restless night, Elly entered the kitchen to help with breakfast. "We missed you at supper last night," Mrs. Branscombe said.

"I'm sorry. I should have let you know. I had some thinking to do," Elly replied.

"That's what we thought. We had a lot of thinking and talking to do too," Mrs. Branscombe said. "We've finally accepted that we can't hold on here. We have to sell off whatever we can, while it's still worth something, and move back to Chicago."

Elly's heart sank. "How soon would you leave?"

"As soon as we can sell what's left of the stock and make sure you're settled."

Elly forced a smile. "Well, I'm glad I'm settled then. I have good news. I got an offer on the wagon and the team. It looks like I'll be headed to Cheyenne with the preachers and a load a freight."

"With the preachers?"

"Yes Ma'am."

"Well I have been praying about you, but it seems God does works in mysterious ways."

*****

Now, two months later here she was, about to leave the kind women and men of the wagon train. With less than a hundred miles to Cheyenne and the only remaining family she had, she would push on and then be done with these men forever.

# Chapter 4

The man, horses, and cattle settled into a routine, but Ogallala could not come soon enough. Thorn led the pack horse well ahead and tied him or, if the grass was good, left him to graze. Then he went back and started the herd west. He shouted and whistled until all the cows and the bull raised their heads. Inevitably one or more cows would cut away and try to stay behind, forcing Thorn and the buckskin to gallop around and push them back to the herd. In the meantime, on the other side of the herd, one or two cows would find their own reasons to stay behind. After much shouting, galloping and bother, the high-horned cow would trail out and the rest of the herd follow. After the midday rest, the whole chaotic scene repeated itself.

Prior to the start of each day's drive and again once the herd was moving well, Thorn rode to high ground and scouted every direction. Only then, did he allow himself to doze in the saddle. Discipline above all else.

At night, he circled his little herd on foot, saving the buckskin for daytime. He sang softly until all the cattle laid down, then he found a high over-watch, where he leaned against his saddle and guarded the herd against Indians, rustlers, and predators.

A few days into the drive, his head bobbed in the warm morning sun. He struggled to hold his eyes open. Every few strides, his chin hit his chest, and he jerked awake. He needed help.

As he topped a small rise, a gray haze floated toward him from the west. Soon he smelled smoke. Powdery gray ash drifted on the wind and floated from the sky, settling on everything. He rode to the highest point around and searched the horizon for flames, but only saw smokey white haze.

The Platte meandered along between his herd and where he imagined the fire to be, but the narrow river would do little to stop a roaring prairie grass fire.

He followed the Oregon trail, but stayed wide of the main track, finding untouched grass for his cattle and avoiding any who may want to take his little herd. Though he was reluctant to expose himself and his herd, with a fire somewhere to the west, he needed information, so he pushed closer to the trail.

After another day in the smoke, he left his cattle grazing and climbed to his chosen guard post. As the sun set, he spotted a campfire further along the trail to the northwest. Once the cattle bedded down and settled in to chew their cuds, he re-saddled the buckskin.

He felt an uncharacteristic hump beneath his saddle. "I know buddy. This is your rest time, but we've gotta find out about that fire." Before long, the buckskin accepted the night ride, and they approached the camp. Thorn circled above the campfire, careful to stay downwind of the horses below. From a hilltop to the northeast he saw four cowboys and eight horses. By the cut of their hats and the wiry ponies they rode, he guessed they were from Texas.

He waited, watched, and listened for over an hour. Finally, he decided that the men were most likely cowboys returning from a drive and not bandits. "Hallo! Can I come in?"

"Come on in," one of the men shouted back, "keep your hands where we can see them."

Thorn rode in to find three men. This was a careful crew. "I'm just hoping for a cup of coffee and some news," he said, keeping his hands visible. "I'm headed to Ogallala and I'm worried about the fire."

"Well I reckon we can help you with both," one cowboy said. "Step down and set a spell. I'm Arlin, that old jasper there is Rufus and the handsome gentleman in the sombrero is Julio." The speaker was short and wiry. He wore a spotted cowhide vest and a flat-brimmed hat. Rufus had gray hair and beard and was the tallest of the three. Julio, obviously a vaquero, wore a sombrero with the front of the brim turned up. All were whip lean and nut brown from months of sun and wind on the trail. All wore pistols in gun belts set high on their hips and free to move with a man on a horse, not low and tied down like want-to-be toughs. The rawhide loops, that kept their pistols in their holsters as they rode, hung lose. The men, though watchful, moved with ease and confidence. The fourth man, out of sight, watched from the shadows.

Cautious, Thorn thought... or dangerous? Resting his hands above his belt buckle, he mentally found his pistol and knife, wanting to be ready, should the need arise. He listened for movement and his ears found the man off to his right. To his left at the edge of his vision, he marked a tree, a tree large enough, should the need arise, to shield him from bullets. "Marshall's my name, Thorn Marshall," he said, all senses alert.

"Never heard of nobody called Thorn," Arlin said, laughing as he offered Thorn a cup of fragrant steaming coffee. "No offense, but you do look a little prickly." The other men snickered.

Thorn took the coffee with his left hand and returned Arlin's smile, "It's Swedish. After my grandfather."

Thorn searched from face to face for signs of danger but found only normal caution.

"Tell your friend to come in. I'm alone and I mean no harm."

Arlin laughed. "Come on in Bobby Jon. I reckon it's okay." Then turning to Thorn, "Fellars can't be too careful. Looks like you feel the same way." Bobby Jon strolled in carrying a rifle.

Thorn nodded and grinned. He liked this crew. "What can you tell me about all this smoke?" Arlin turned and motioned south and west with his hands. "Big grass fire burning everything in sight around

Ogallala. We was told the railroad started it and they're trying to back burn to get it stopped 'fore it gets into Ogallala or crosses the Platte." His eyes sparkled as he spoke. "Glad we got our cows to Bozeman. A fire like this could take all the grass out of this country."

"You were in Bozeman?" Thorn asked, his voice urgent and interested. "I hear it's fine country."

"No place prettier, especially east of there along the Yellowstone," Rufus replied. There's rolling hills, lots of grass, and all the water a man or cow needs.

Arlin grinned at another opportunity to perform. "There's deer and elk for the taking and the river is full of trout and most the range is still open. If it weren't for Indians and long winters, it'd be as close to heaven as a cowboy and a cow could get. Least this side of the pearly gates."

Thorn had an idea. These Texas boys knew the trail and were obviously cowmen. "Would a couple of you boys be interested in going back north? I know of a little herd of purebreds, heading up to the Yellowstone River country, that could use a couple of good hands who've been over the trail."

All the cowboys shook their heads. "I reckon we been away from home long enough," Arlin said. "Sides, a feller going this late would have to spend the winter and we ain't got the clothes nor the blood for that."

"You'll have a hard time finding drovers between here and that country," Bobby Jon added. "Your best bet would have been Ogallala, but now you might find men in Cheyenne. There ain't much for people once you get further north."

"You tell them boys with that herd they better get

a move on," Rufus said. "They say winter comes hard and early up there, but I reckon if a fella got there in time to scout a good spot, them cows would make it through on the side slopes where the wind blows the snow off. Feller would need a cabin though and plenty of firewood."

Thorn finished his coffee and set the cup on a rock by the fire. He hadn't realized how lonely he was, until he'd spent an hour with these lively Texas cowboys, but he had a herd to tend. "I guess I'd better cut a trail."

"You and your horse look rode hard," Rufus said. "You're welcome to spend the night here. We still got a chunk a bacon."

"I've got a little camp already set up, but I do appreciate the news and the coffee," and with that, he mounted and rode northwest out of camp. Once out of earshot of the cowboys, he circled back to his herd.

The cattle checked, and the buckskin rubbed down and picketed, Thorn wrapped himself in his blanket and huddled into a little patch of brush on top of the hill overlooking his herd. He didn't sleep that night. Those Texas boys seemed alright, but they were mighty watchful. Maybe that's how they grew 'em down there. A soldier could never be too careful.

Thorn felt more pressed for after talking to the Texans. He decided to avoid Ogallala and go north and west away from the fire, then cut back to Cheyenne to find men. It would add more long and tiring days and nights, but it seemed the wise choice.

Thorn pushed the cattle harder. He needed to get out of the path of the fire, and he needed to find someone to share the watch, so he could get some sleep. He'd traveled northwest staying on the fringe of the Oregon Trail. Now he needed to cross the North Platte and go west and south to hit Cheyenne.

Though he no longer rode in the smoke, he checked often for fire. The smoke appeared to be moving north toward him, but with most of the wind coming from the west, he hoped to be by it, before it cut his path.

Just after midday, the wind picked up. As he topped a small hill, Thorn saw trouble in the distance. His heart raced as he thought the fire had come north, but he couldn't smell smoke and the swirls and flashes of white made him wonder if it was a snowstorm. He'd been warned that snow could come anytime in this part of the world. Satisfied that it wasn't fire, but not waiting to figure out what it was, he pushed his cattle into a little grove of trees, surrounding a small spring. He unsaddled his horses and picketed them. Though he had been camping under the stars, he took his well-oiled ground sheet and tied it between two small cottonwoods.

With everything tied down, he picked up his rifle and climbed to the rim of the coulee. He could see the storm flashing and shimmering toward him, swirling and eddying silver and gray from horizon to horizon. Snow, he wondered again? Maybe, but the wind was warm and dry.

As the cloud drew closer, it crackled and hissed like a prairie fire, but the smell and color was wrong. Then they were on him. Grasshoppers. Locust. First, a few bounced off of him, then hundreds, then thousands, millions, billions and the sky was dark.

Thorn bounded down the hill shielding his eyes, tucking his rifle under his arm so he could grab his shirt collar, to keep the beasts from crawling in. Close to panic, his horses whinnied and pranced at the end of their picket ropes. Prickly legs and the ever-chewing jaws rasped at his skin.

Thankfully the cattle had moved deep into the brush and lay down, eyes closed and heads down. Thorn grabbed his horses and pulled them in, heads against the tarp and calmed them with soothing words, as he brushed the vermin from their faces. Despite the flapping tarp, the horses huddled closer. He tore off his shirt and whisked the bugs from around his waist and from his armpits where they chewed the hairs. He shook the shirt and struggled to get it back on without letting more insects inside.

As the swarm settled down to devour anything edible they could find, they smothered everything in layer upon layer of scratching, writhing, ever-chewing life. Thorn pulled his gear closer under the tarp and saw that the beasts were chewing the fleece from the bottom of his saddle, the wool of his Navajo saddle blanket and the mohair of his cinches.

He grabbed the saddle blanket, beat the insects into the dirt and swept them away, with his boots. The horses fell back in fear, then unable to stand the locusts bouncing off their faces, they ignored the thrashing blanket and pushed their heads back in against the tarp. Thorn continued beating and sweeping until a three-foot high berm of dead and dying locust surrounded him.

For hours, he kept up the battle, until arms too weak and too heavy to swing the blanket, he slumped to the ground. The locust kept coming. In desperation, he gathered all his gear into a pile and scooped handful after handful of the sticky corpses, until everything of value was covered in an oozing mound of dead insects. He then loosened half of the tarp and wrapped himself, covering his head. The warmth of the sun and the scratchy hum of the locust on the tarp soon lulled him to sleep.

When he awoke, the sun was up, and the sky was clear. Though the ground was still covered in crawling locusts, the majority of the swarm had moved on with the wind. Still tied near the tarp, his horses, with nothing else to eat, nibbled at the insects, chewing and crunching the brittle bodies with relish. Not seeing his cattle, Thorn leapt to his feet and ran up the draw. The cattle were a few hundred yards down the coulee, also feeding on the insects.

Looking around, he saw nothing but shades of brown. The locust had eaten everything green, every blade of grass, every leaf and even the small branches from the brush behind him. Thorn pulled his saddle and other equipment from the pile of dead locust. Despite the sticky brown slime on everything, his cinches, bridles and other tack, were intact, as was his food. He opened every pocket, container and cleaned the bugs from every hiding spot. He checked his canteens. They were whole, and the water was fine.

Thinking of his animals, he checked the spring. Sweeping away a layer of locust, he found the water in the little pool brown and foul. He tasted it and spit it from his mouth. He led his horses over. Though they had not had a drink for over a day, they sniffed the water and turned away.

Returning to camp, he decided to try to filter some water through his bandana. Sweeping the locust from the pool, he noticed a corner where the water looked clearer. On closer inspection, rivulets of clear water bubbled from the earth and snaked out through the brown water of the pool. Careful not to plug the little spring, he scooped handfuls of mud from the bottom and built a dike around the area. Before long he had a pool of sweet clean water. This time when he brought the horses over, they drank deeply. As soon as the horses finished the cattle moved in and drank.

During the war, whenever trouble hit their little band of raiders, the Colonel had quoted another of his favorites, Marcus Aurelius, saying: 'You've got to accept the things to which fate binds you.'

Now, he needed to know exactly what faced him. He saddled his horse and rode to the highest point of land. As far as he could see, the devastation was complete; not a speck of green. He was in trouble. Fate had bound him days from any town, no feed, maybe no water, and everything he owned tied up in this drive.

With no way of knowing how wide a swath the locust had cut, he couldn't even guess which direction to go to find feed. With the fire to the south and moving north, he couldn't go there. To go back and find clean water in the North Platte, would increase the risk of being hit by the fire. He had to press on, force march the cattle to Cheyenne. They could make it with no feed, but if all the water in the path of the locust plague was fouled, they would die.

He wanted to curl under his tarp and sleep, but instead, he tied his pack horse to a spindly, chewed up tree, a quarter mile southwest and started the cattle moving toward Cheyenne.

# Chapter 5

A few miles west, Elly and her so-called business partners also skirted the fire. The first night camping, away from the friendly comfort of the families in the wagon train, left her fearful of the rest of the trip. As soon as the wagon stopped, the men opened one of the wooden crates of whiskey—the freight they had purchased.

Wilf pulled the cork with his teeth and spit it onto the ground. "It's nice to have a drink without having to hide it from that pack of sod busters." He drank, wiped the mouth of the bottle on his sleeve, and extended it toward Elly.

Over the years, Elly had seen whiskey makers come into her father's store for bags of sugar and yeast. Many showed the ravages of enjoying their products to excess, but none compared to the couple who'd sold the whiskey to the preachers. The old man had a hunched back and hobbled along leaning on a sturdy branch. He had a few strands of wispy gray hair and he constantly wiped his red, bulbous nose with his arm. His eyes were pale, almost white, and tears trickled constantly from the corners. The old woman shuffled along as if in pain, but she cackled and giggled at everything anyone said to her. She wore a dress, so filthy it was impossible to tell what color it had once been. Elly could not imagine drinking anything those two prepared.

"No thank you," she replied. Her father had rarely taken a drink, and she had never learned to be comfortable around drunk men. "I'm not a drinker."

"You're missing out. We need to learn ya to have some fun," Herb said. "Even the good Lord liked to get his drink on. Turned water into wine."

"If we could do that, we'd be rich," Wilf said with a chuckle.

"And happy," Herb said, as he tipped the bottle. "Goddamn!" he exclaimed, passing the bottle to Herb. "I reckon the wine the Good Lord made woulda been better than this cat piss."

Wilf shuddered as he took a drink. "It'll be just fine for the red skinned heathens."

Herb laughed and stretched out his hand. "Pass 'er back here. Any port in a storm, my daddy used to say." While the men drank, Elly tended to the team and made a supper of biscuits and beans.

"Supper," she called, hoping to end the drinking.

"I reckon I ain't gonna ruin a two-dollar drunk on a two bit meal," Herb said.

"Fine. I'll leave it here if you want it," she said, as she took her plate and sat on a rock on the other side of the wagon. Her meal done, she packed away the food and climbed under the wagon and into her bedroll.

"Play us a tune Wilf," Herb said. Wilf pulled out his harmonica and played a refrain of "Dixie." "Play the bathing song,"

Herb laughed and then started to sing in his beautiful voice:

The four and twentieth day of May, of all days of the
year, sir,
A virgin lady, fresh and gay, did privately appear, sir.
Hard by a riverside got she, and did sing loud, the
rather,
For she was sure she was secure, and had intent to
bath her.
With glittering glancing jealous eyes, she shyly looks
about, sir,
To see if any lurking spies were hid to find her out,
sir.
And being well resolved that none could see her
nakedness, sir,
She pulled her robes off, one by one, and did herself
undress, sir.
Into the fluent stream she leapt, she looked like
Venus' glass, sir.
The fishes from all quarters crept to see so fair a lass,
sir.
Each fish did wish himself a man, about her all were
drawn, sir.
And at the sight of her began to spread about their

spawn, sir.
A lad that long her love had been and could obtain no
grace, sir,
For all her prying lay unseen, hid in a secret place, sir.
Who had often been repulsed when he had come to
woo her,
Pulled off his clothes and furiously did run and leap
into her.
She squeaked, she cried, and down she dived, he
brought her up again, sir.
He brought her up upon the shore, and then, and
then, and then, sir.
As Adam did old Eve enjoy, you may guess what I
mean, sir;
Because she all uncovered lay, he covered her again,
sir.
With watered eyes, she pants and cries, "I'm utterly
undone, sir,
If you will not be wed to me by the next morning
sun, sir."
He answered her, he would not stir out of her sight
till then, sir.
We'll both clasp hands in wedlock bands, marry, and
to it again, sir.

The men roared with drunken laughter as the song
ended. Elly pulled the bedroll over her head and wept
into her sleeve.

The next morning, without the noise of the larger
group to wake them, the men slept well past first
light. Afraid to wake them, but anxious to get on the
trail, Elly watered and harnessed the team and
prepared a breakfast of biscuits and bacon. The men
awoke, the smell of last night's whiskey wafting from
every pore. Wilf rubbed his temples with the knuckles

of both hands. "I reckon we better go easy on them crates for the rest of the trip or we ain't gonna have no profit."

To Elly's surprise, the men were in good humor. With her preparations, they were fast on the trail, would soon be one day closer to Cheyenne. As midday approached, Elly drove the team, while the men dozed on top of the crates in the wagon box. As they topped a small rise, hoping to find water, or at least a good spot for the horses to graze, she scanned around for a stopping place. To the south, she saw the huge plumes of smoke still rising and blowing north and west on a stiff breeze. To the west she saw what looked like a huge whirlwind. "Wake Up," she said. "Wake up! There's something coming. I think it's a tornado. We've got to find shelter."

The men jumped from the wagon bed and seeing the danger, sprinted around and sprang to the seat on either side of Elly. Wilf took the reins and slapped the team, pushing them into a fast trot.

"Over there," Elly pointed at a grove of small trees, as they topped the rise. The storm flashed and swirled closer, sparkling in the midday sun.

Before they could reach the trees, the front edge of the swarm dropped from the sky and locusts started hitting them, some bouncing off and some grabbing hold with their stickery legs. "Git 'em off me," Herb shouted, waving his arms frantically, as Wilf stopped the team at the edge of the trees. The horses snorted, stamped their feet, shook and swished their tails, trying to rid themselves of the hoppers.

"Get down and get their heads," Wilf shouted at Herb. "Elly and I will unhitch the traces." Elly jumped down beside the off horse and grabbed the chain links holding the big horse to the wagon. The horse lurched ahead taking the slack and making it impossible to unhook the heavy wagon.

"Push 'em back," Wilf screamed over the racket! Herb held the two horses with one hand and swept locusts from his face with the other. As the wind gust died down, the locusts started dropping en masse. Herb clawed at his head with both hands dropping the reins. The big horses bolted, and spun away from the onslaught, knocking Herb and Wilf to the ground and leaving Elly standing, watching as the wagon wheels somehow missed both men, and the horses and wagon thundered off across the prairie.

Elly sprinted across the rough ground. "Whoa! Whoa!" Shielding her eyes with her hands, she ran and called and ran until the horses disappeared behind a wall of locusts, and she could run no more. She dropped to her knees and wept. Everything she had left in the world was in that wagon.

After a moment of tears, Elly climbed to her feet and started marching east after the team.

"Where you going Miss Elly?" Wilf shouted. "That team's long gone."

Without looking back, she walked on.

*****

Further east, Thorn plodded along, leading the buckskin. The cattle and horses carried enough flesh to make the trek on limited grass. Water was the problem. With nothing green to mark them, Thorn feared he may not find the springs he depended on for his livestock. Without the temptation of green grass, the cattle lined out quickly, the high-horned cow leading the way. Each hoof fall kicked up a puff of dust under the hot sun.

Instead of wasting time hunting springs, Thorn decided to push straight to Wild Woman Creek. As best he could calculate, the creek was twenty miles, or a little more, to the south east, a long, hard push, but the best chance for finding water, and the route led directly toward Cheyenne.

At midday, he stopped to rest the animals. The cattle and horses picked at the sparse, dry grass. Finding almost nothing to eat, the cattle bawled and continued moving forward on their own. Thorn led his horses to a high point, to keep an eye on the cattle while the horses rested.

In the distance, to his west, a flock of crows circled, fell, rose and fell again. Something was dead or dying. The crows lunch was none of his business. It was probably nothing more than an antelope or some other prairie animal, dead from old age. Even if it was a man, if the crows were there, he was already dead or dying.

On second thought, the Colonel would have sent a scouting party. He understood the importance of knowing one's surroundings. If Indians or outlaws had killed someone or something, he needed to know. After resting an hour, Thorn caught up to the herd and pushed them in the general direction of the crows. Before he got too close, he left the cattle in a low spot and rode closer. The crows continued to rise and fall. Whomever or whatever it was, had not died yet.

He crawled to the brow of a hill, keeping his head down. Across the shallow valley at the bottom of a gray, clay cliff, a team of black horses lay under the smashed remains of a wagon. A crow landed on the belly of one of the horses. The horse kicked feebly, sending the crow back into flight. There were no people anywhere in sight. A flash of movement caught his eye and half-a-mile northeast, a pack of gray prairie wolves trotted along the skyline.

Thorn drove his cattle closer to the team and wagon. Two big black Percheron geldings lay under the shattered front wheels and seat of a freight wagon. As he rode close, they raised their heads and tried to rise, but the tangle of harness and the weight of the wagon kept them down.

"Easy boys. Easy," Thorn said, as he approached, his rifle cocked and in hand. "What happened. Let's get you out of there. How'd you get here?" He chattered softly expecting no answers but trying to calm the horses. The remains of the wagon lay across the hips and bellies of the horses. The tongue had broken free of the wagon, but the trace chains were still attached to the double tree, tying the horses to the remains of the heavy wagon. Reaching over the horses backs to avoid being kicked, he unhooked the traces.

He scanned for something to pry the wagon off the horses, but the pole was broken and there was no other long lever. "I gotta get you boys up," he said. He leaned a shoulder under the heavy remains of the wagon and pushed. At first, nothing moved. He lowered his hips, pushed his shoulder deeper and heaved. Inch by inch he straightened his legs. He gasped for air. Sweat dripped from his face. He refused to give in to the burning in his thighs and lungs until the wreckage reached a tipping point and toppled away from the horses. He slumped to the ground, hooked an arm over the bright red, brass-tipped hames of the top horse, and leaned against the broad black backs.

Once he caught his breath, Thorn stood and unhooked the bridle rein, freeing the top horse from the horse on the bottom. He pulled the big head back toward the horse's hip. The horse tried to rise, but fell back panting. Doubling the rein, Thorn whipped the horse over and over until it scrambled to its feet and stood panting on three legs. Its right rear hoof dangled from its hock, held only by tendon and skin, the cannon bone shattered. The horse lurched forward, then stopped, its sides heaving.

With the weight of the wagon and the top horse gone, the bottom horse struggled to rise. Thorn grabbed the bridle and encouraged the gelding. "Come on boy, get up." First, the big horse thrust its forelegs out front and then raised its big black head. Mighty muscles flexed, but the gelding only rose halfway, dragging himself along the ground, hips and hind legs unable to move.

Thorn pulled his knife. Someone owned these horses and could be near. He could not risk the noise of a shot. The big horse swayed back and forth on its front legs, hind legs splayed to either side, frozen to the ground. "Easy boy. Easy," he chanted, as he covered the horse's left eye and steadied the big head. He gently placed the knife tip into the hollow where the horse's jaw met its neck. Before the horse could react, he plunged the sharp knife through and out and down. Bright red-hot blood covered his hand and gushed to the ground. For a moment, the great gelding teetered, then slumped into the spreading puddle of his own blood.

Without wiping the blade, Thorn approached the standing horse that now trembled with shock and snorted at the smell of blood. "Sorry boy," Thorn said, as he petted the horse until it let him cover its left eye. "I wish there was another way," he said, as he plunged the knife in and danced back, out of the reach of flailing hooves and the falling horse.

As the horses choked out their last breaths, Thorn looked around. Under the seat, he found three bedrolls. Three people, he thought. He tied the rolls on top of his pack horse's load, using one of the long bridle reins from the team. Before leaving the big horses to the crows and wolves, he cut a strip of meat from one loin, wrapped it in his bandana and tied it behind his saddle, over his own bedroll.

Gathering his horses and cattle, Thorn found a path around the bluffs. Once on top, he saw wagon tracks heading straight west through the dry prairie grass. He wondered what had driven the team here to die, so far off the Oregon trail and away from any settlement. The locust? Could be. Indians? No, Indians were practical and would have taken the horse meat and the blankets. Whatever caused the runaway, the people at the end of the wagon track were dead or in serious trouble. In spite of his need to find water for his cattle, Thorn headed west, pushing along the wagon tracks, instead of southwest to Wild Woman Creek.

'Pay attention and a man's backtrail will tell you as much about a man,' the Colonel had once told him, 'as you can learn by watching him.'

Thorn stepped from the buckskin and opened a heavy canvas bag, lying on the dry prairie grass. Inside, simple, clean dresses and frilly things spoke of a woman. He would have brought the clothes along, had his pack horse not already been heavily laden. If the woman lived, she would want these things.

As small dressing table and broken mirror confirmed there was a woman. Thorn stepped from the saddle and untied the cord from around the drawer in the table and slid it open. He unwrapped a carefully packaged, framed tintype picture of a man with a dark mustache. The man stood between a beautiful woman, wisps of fair hair hanging in her face, and a tall boy around fourteen. The woman's left hand rested on the shoulder of a lovely light-haired girl child of around ten.

Thorn stared at the picture, then held it briefly to his chest. It could have been his own family, had they lived a few more years. Someone had taken care packing this picture and would want it. He carefully re-wrapped it and tucked it into his saddle bag. Deeper in the drawer, behind several books, he found two leather drawstring bags. The smaller held two gold bands, one large and one small, and a gold, tree-shaped, pendant on a fine gold chain. The larger bag held a double eagle and a few greenbacks. Thorn tucked both pouches in beside the picture. Someone's treasures.

Further along, he picked up a bag of flour and a full side of bacon. He brushed away the beetles devouring it, then he smelled whiskey and came across ten smashed crates of mostly broken whiskey bottles. He picked up an unbroken bottle, twisted out the cork, sniffed the contents and took a small sip. He spat it from his mouth. Firewater! Pepper—and Lord only knows what else—laced whiskey distilled and mixed for Indians and the poorest workers. Only the lowest kind of traders trucked in this swill.

Thorn kicked apart the crates, then pulled out his rifle and used the butt to smash any unbroken bottles. He considered turning his herd back southwest, but there was still the woman and the picture.

He passed a broken water barrel, a broken wagon wheel and then, as he cautiously topped a small rise, he saw them. A half mile west, a woman and two men, arms laden, walked toward him. He pulled his rifle from its scabbard and lay it across the pommel of his saddle.

As he got closer, one of the men shouted, "Hello! Did ya come across our team and wagon?"

"I did," Thorn replied, as he rode closer. "They're gone."

"What do you mean gone?" the taller man asked.

"Dead gone." Thorn jerked his horse to a stop. He knew the men! His fist clenched tightly around the stock of his rifle. Torture and murder flashed behind his eyes. Instead of killing them, then and there, he pulled his hat low over his eyes and swung his rifle toward them. "That's close enough."

"What's wrong?" the shorter man asked. "I reckon we ain't done nothing to cross you."

*****

When Thorn still served the Colonel as a boy servant, these two men rode with his band of red legged raiders. Among men who murdered and stole in the name of God, Country, and the Union, these two were the worst; raiders who chafed at every order and brought unwanted attention to the group with their unbridled savagery.

The one thing the Colonel did not tolerate was rape. He believed wars were to be fought by and between men. He allowed, even encouraged his men to kill any woman who raised a weapon against them, but women who surrendered or hid were to be left alone.

During raids and battles, Thorn ferried ammunition and ran other errands. He carried a pistol, but was not expected to use it, except in his own defense. After a bloody day, watching murder and pillage, Thorn ducked into the town livery to clear his head. There, he walked in on Wilf holding a sobbing young woman's hands over a saddle rack, while Herb thrust into her from behind. He darted out, but not before Wilf saw him.

By the time he returned with the Colonel, the men and the woman were gone. When confronted, the men denied ever being in the stable.

The raiders had lost four men that day, their worst loss ever, and the Colonel allowed the men to stay. Despite their shortcomings, they fought like lions and the Colonel desperately needed men.

The two said nothing to Thorn about what he saw, until months later on a bored and drunken day, the Colonel gone from camp, they horsewhipped him. Wilf held him over a wagon tongue while Rat-Faced Herb swung the buggy whip.

When the Colonel rode into camp and found Thorn whipped and bleeding, he disarmed the two men, handed his and their weapons to his second in command.

Wilf and Herb were soldiers and brawlers, and years younger than the Colonel, but he took them on at the same time. Thorn watched, standing beside the second in command, Captain Wren Howard. Wilf and Herb fought as if possessed by demons; they fought for their very lives. At one point, Herb jumped on the Colonel's back pinning his arms. Wilf struck the leader a vicious blow to the chin and the Colonel's legs buckled.

Thorn started forward. Captain Wren grabbed his shoulder and held him back. "He's still got this," the captain said. Instead, of going down, the Colonel threw himself forward, hurling Herb from his back. Finding reserves, deep within himself, he delivered punch and kick after punch and kick to the two men, until they lay at his feet and begged for mercy. By the time the Colonel finished, his arms and face were covered in blood, much his, but more theirs. Though he wasn't a big man, he grabbed both men by their collars and dragged them together to the edge of the camp.

"I should have done this long ago," he said, in his heavy European accent. "If I ever see either of you again, I won't be so gentle."

"That's the God-carved-in-stone-damndest fighting man I've ever seen," the captain said. "Your a lucky boy."

Waves of joy ran up and down Thorn's body. He had never felt happier. That day marked a turning point. "I never want that to happen again," the Colonel said. As soon as he had recovered, he began training Thorn in the arts of war mastered in a lifetime as a mercenary, both in Europe and America: rifles and pistols, French savate, boxing, and wrestling, sabers, rapiers and lances. He taught him military theory and tactics, and the importance of courage. 'All men feel fear,' the Colonel often said.

'Brave men feel it and still do what needs to be done.'

\*\*\*\*\*

Wanting to see if they recognized him, Thorn pushed back his hat and rode closer, his rifle casually pointed toward the men. The taller man cradled a rifle in his arms, had a sheepskin coat over his shoulder and several boxes of ammunition in his hand. He wore a pistol on a belt strapped tightly over bib overalls. "Do we know you?" he asked.

"I don't know. Do you?"

"I don't think we do stranger. But why're ya so unfriendly?" the smaller man asked. He also carried a rifle, boxes of ammunition and a canvas sack in his arms. "You do look familiar. Do you know us?"

For years, Thorn had dreamed of meeting these men and paying them back for, both the things that they had done to him, and the terrible things he has seen them do. Now he found them, the worst men he had ever encountered, traveling with a seemingly respectable young woman. Something was off, and he needed to find out what. He lowered the rifle toward the ground but kept it pointed in the direction of the men.

"No, I don't recognize you."

"We got enough problems. Help us or just leave us be," the small man whined, inching the barrel of his rifle toward Thorn.

"Keep them rifles pointed at the ground," Thorn said, raising his rifle and showing them the dark bore of the barrel.

"Excuse our impoliteness," the woman said, with a soft Missouri drawl. "I'm Eloise Strong." Despite the dirt on her face and her windblown hair, she was the most beautiful woman Thorn had ever seen. She carried her tall, slim frame with dignity. Her sparkling, green eyes looked directly into Thorn's. "These are my business partners," she said, "Wilf," pointing to the taller man, "and Herb," pointing to the other. "Did you say our horses are dead?" The sun sparkled red gold in her hair.

Thorn hesitated, momentarily tongue tied. "Yes ma'am. I had to put them down. They went over a cliff. They were bad hurt."

She looked, sounded, and acted like a proper woman.

"Our wagon?"

"Broken to pieces I'm afraid." What could she be doing with these two? Had she said business partners? She slumped, and the sparkle left her eyes.

Wilf stepped to one side, stretched to his full height, and cupped a hand over his eyes. "Our freight?"

"You can probably smell the rot gut in Kansas City," Thorn replied, not surprised that Wilf and Herb would stoop to trading rot gut to the Indians.

"Damn, that was for trading! Where's the rest of your outfit?" Wilf asked. "Your cook and such?"

"I'm traveling alone."

"Alone? Drivin' them funny looking cows? Just look at that bull. He looks like a red buffaler with a white face. What do you mean alone?" Herb said.

"Alone, alone. I'm driving these Hereford cattle to Cheyenne. I'll pick up help there to drive them north."

"Could we travel with you?" the woman asked. "We're headed to Cheyenne as well."

She doesn't seem to be a captive, Thorn thought, but a business partner? "I won't leave you here," Thorn said, stepping down, keeping his horse between him and the men. "Just put those rifles down men and let's have a little chat."

Why are you so unfriendly," Wilf asked? "We mean you no harm. We're good Christian folks. The good Lord said we should all be like the good Samaritan and help a poor traveler we find beaten and starving at the side of the road."

"I guess I don't like people trading whiskey to the Indians," Thorn said, to keep them from guessing the real reason.

"The Lord himself turned water to wine," Wilf stated. "There's nothing wrong with sharing the Lord's goodness with the savages."

Thorn forced his eyes away, took his canteen from the saddle, and passed it to the woman.

She took a sip and passed it to Wilf. "Can we gather more of our belongings?" she asked.

"You can, but I don't know how you would carry any more and these cattle need water, so I'll soon be headed to Wild Woman Creek."

"Did you perchance see a small wooden dressing table?"

"Check that right saddlebag ma'am. I did pick up a couple of things."

Elly unbuckled the straps. She first pulled out the picture, looked at it and hugged it to her breast. "Thank you. Thank you, Mister....?"

Thorn hesitated. "Kansas. You can call me Kansas." "Alright, Mr. Kansas," she replied, a quizzical look on her face.

"Just Kansas, Miss. There's no need for the Mister.

There's more in there."

She pulled out the small pouch next, loosened the drawstring and poured the rings and the pendant into her hand. Tears welled in her eyes.

"The other pouch is in there too… nothing's been bothered," Thorn said. "You can leave them there for now if you like. I promise they'll be safe."

"Thank you. Thank you for bringing me my things. You must have suffered losses yourself."

"I'm sure we all have Miss Eloise. I'm glad I found them."

She smiled, but there was no joy in her eyes. "Call me Elly."

Herb walked over and handed Thorn the empty canteen. Thorn saw red. "What kind of fool guzzles a full canteen, when we don't know where the next water is?"

"I thought you said we was headin' to Wild Woman Creek," Herb stammered. "'Sides we ain't drank since them horses run off."

"And you may not drink tomorrow if the creek's dry. And I said I'm going to Wild Woman Creek. I suggest you folks go back where ever you came from. It's bound to be a hard march to Cheyenne from here, with no feed for these cattle and horses…"

"But we've got nothing," Wilf whined.

Thorn untied the flour and bacon from his saddle and tossed them on the ground at Herb's feet. "The bacon and flour's yours anyway." Then he pulled another canteen from his pack saddle and dropped it on the bacon. "I won't leave you dry, but you may want to save some of that."

"Well I guess we're headed to Cheyenne too," Wilf said.

Thorn wanted to tell the men they could go to Hell and help them to get there, but there was the woman. She could never be safe with these two.

Elly placed a gentle hand on Thorn's knee. "I've nothing to go back to. My only hope is to get to Cheyenne. Please let us travel with you. We won't be a burden."

The Colonel always told Thorn to keep his friends close and his enemies closer, so despite all his misgivings, he decided it would be safer to let them travel with him, than to have them following along on their own. This way, he could keep an eye on them until he figured things out. "I imagine you will," Thorn said mostly to himself, before stepping down and picking up the canteen, bacon and flour from the ground and tying them back on his saddle. He remounted. "Come on then."

# Chapter 6

When they pushed the herd over the last rise and dropped into Wild Woman Creek, the sun had set and a thin crescent of twilight provided the only light. Relief washed over Thorn. A rivulet of water trickled along the rocky stream bed. Smelling it, the cattle broke into a trot. Though foot sore from walking most of the day, Herb and Wilf ran past the cattle and dropped face-first into the stream, forcing the cattle to move around them. Elly rode the buckskin and led the pack horse while Thorn walked along behind.

Thorn reached up and helped Elly from the saddle.

"Go ahead upstream and drink. I'll tend to the horses."

"I'll help," she said, leading the saddle horse to the stream bank, where he drank deeply. She's game, Thorn thought, and she's thinking of the animals before herself. He smiled and let the pack horse drink while he unloaded him.

"You men set up this tarp and get a fire going. Not too big," Thorn said, taking the canteens.

Herb spit a stream of tobacco juice, then wiped his beard with the palm of his hand and wiped his hand on the brown stain on the front of his shirt. "Your awful bossy for a boy barely dry behind the ears. The good Lord said to respect your elders."

"A good man earns respect," Thorn replied. These two hadn't changed.

"I remember hearing that before," Wilf mumbled scratching his chin, as Thorn turned and stomped upstream to fill the canteens.

While Elly made biscuits, Thorn cooked slices of horse meat in bacon fat he had saved. The smell of the campfire, biscuits baking, and meat sizzling in the bacon fat had Thorn's mouth watering. When the food was ready, he passed the frying pan of sizzling meat to Elly.

"No thank you," she said.

"You need to eat," Thorn said. "Please. Help yourself."

"More for us." Herb said, scooping a plateful of meat and sopping his biscuit in the drippings. As the men wolfed down the meal, Thorn placed one of his biscuits on Elly's plate. She picked it up and handed it back, but he stopped her hand and looked her in the eye.

"You walked a long way today, and we've got another long walk tomorrow." Elly nodded and took the biscuit. After supper, Elly scrubbed the dishes with sand from the creek. Thorn took a clean frying pan of water and doused the fire. Steam, ash, and smoke billowed into the air with a sharp hiss.

"What are you doing?" Herb asked.

"It's getting cold," Wilf said.

"We're in Indian country," Thorn replied, getting another pan of water and stirring it in until the fire was dead.

Wilf glared. "You're mighty uppity, boy."

"Feels like we're back in the army," Herb said. "You look so familiar. You sure we ain't met? You fight in the war?"

"He's hardly old enough," said Wilf. "But…"

Thorn bit his tongue and squeezed his hands together, then gathered up his bedroll, and headed out of camp. "I'll take the watch," he said. "I haven't been sleeping much anyway. I'll be up on the hill." He needed time and space alone to think and figure things out.

He looked at his cattle, the two men, and the woman. After all these years, fate had stuck him with helping his tormentors. Why hadn't they recognized him? It was only a matter of time. He'd been a late bloomer, and when the men were driven from the Colonel's company, he was still a boy, small with white blonde hair. Now his hair was a dark dirty blonde, and he had a full beard. He needed to avoid talking about the past, especially anything to do with the Colonel or the war. He had already slipped a couple of times. He would be more careful. "When the time's right, I'll let you boys know who I am," he whispered, "and then there will be hell to pay."

A few hours later, Thorn struggled to hold his eyes open. Watching over the cattle day and night had worn him thin, and sharing his horse and watching the men had robbed him of the little naps, he had been taking during the day. He wanted to let his eyes close, just rest them a few seconds, but he knew if he did, he would fall asleep. He couldn't let that happen.

Hungry, the cattle took turns standing, milling around, and laying back down. He worried that something other than hunger might be bothering them. Below, Elly rose, wrapped her blanket over her shoulders, and started up toward him. "I can't sleep," she said, as she approached.

Thorn chuckled. "And I can barely stay awake."

"Thank you for bringing my things," she said.

"I'm glad I found them. A person should have things to remember by. I wish I did," he said yawning.

"You seem honest," she said, her green eyes staring into his. "Should I worry that you don't use your real name?"

Thorn thought for a moment. "No, I don't think you should," he said, with the slightest emphasis on the 'you.'

"Well then, I'll leave it at that for now," she said, placing a hand on his arm. He liked her touch. He started to warn her about the men, but he choked back the words. He had to be sure first.

"Sleep," she said. "I'll watch. If I see or hear anything. I'll wake you."

"Anything at all," he warned. "Everything I own is down there."

"Me too."

"Even if your partners come up."

Elly looked at him and waited. When he said nothing, she said, "I will. I promise."

He believed her, and for the first time in days, he truly slept.

At first light, Thorn saddled the buckskin and led him to Elly.

Wilf limped toward the horse. "I need to ride first. My feet hurt. My boots ain't made for walking all this way."

Thorn kept walking toward Elly. "They're my horses and the lady will ride first."

Elly touched his arm again and said, "It's alright, I'll walk along behind with you."

Still angry, but liking the idea of Elly's company, Thorn handed the reins to Wilf. "Ride out front. That lead cow will follow the horse. And keep a sharp eye."

Wilf bristled. "I know how to be watchful. I was a soldier before you were born, boy."

Thorn bit his tongue. Anything he might say, risked reminding the men of his identity. Without talking, Thorn, Elly and Herb walked along behind the herd.

"I reckon I'll leave you two love birds here to eat dust. I'm a gonna get upwind of these stinkin' critters," Herb said.

Once Herb was out of earshot, Thorn said, "Can I ask you a question?

She met his eyes and nodded.

"How did you fall in with these two? They don't seem like your kind."

"I'm beginning to wonder myself," she said. "After Momma died, all I had left of value was the team and wagon and what you found in my dressing table. Those black geldings were my father's pride and joy.

He used them to haul his own freight for our store. With the war taking my father and brother, we had no work for the team, but Momma couldn't bear to part with them."

Seeing and feeling the pain in her eyes, he now understood why she refused to eat the meat. He wouldn't eat the buckskin either, unless he was starving, and the big blacks meant even more to her. He wished he'd been able to save them.

"After Momma passed, my Aunt invited me to come and live with them in Cheyenne. I tried to sell the team, but no one back home had cash money to buy them. Wilf and Herb were preachers."

"Preachers?" Thorn asked. "Those two?"

"Yes," she replied, "snake charming preachers."

"Preachers? Wonders never cease."

"Now that I know them, I believe the preaching was just a way to get easy money."

"Sounds right."

"They offered me safe passage to Cheyenne and a quarter interest in their freight business, in return for the team and wagon. Wilf even offered to have the lawyer draw up paper so it would all be legal. I had to get to Cheyenne while I still had money, so before I could change my mind, I agreed."

Thorn was still thinking of her saying she had lost her father, brother and mother. "What side were they on?" he asked.

"Wilf and Herb?"

"No your father and brother."

"We're from Missouri. We never owned slaves, but my father thought the states should have the right to secede. My brother joined the army."

"What happened?"

"My brother died fighting and when the Red Legs raided Breedlin they murdered my father."

Thorn dropped his head and looked away. She was from Breedlin—and traveling with these two? This couldn't be. He wanted to tell her, then and there, about Wilf and Herb, but his training kicked in and he knew he couldn't risk it, not until he was a hundred percent sure he could trust her to not confront the men, and until he was ready to deal with them. He realized that once she knew, she would want nothing more to do with any of them, including him. He had just met her, but his heart ached at the thought of her hating him.

Now that he knew, he would do whatever it took to keep her safe—to give her back some kind of life. He owed her that.

# Chapter 7

Before he could say more, Wilf galloped back. "Soldiers coming! They're riding hard from the north."

"Get off," Thorn said, taking his horse in hand. "I'll go meet them."

"I can talk to them," Wilf said.

"Get off my horse."

Wilf glared as he swung his leg over the cantle and stepped to the ground. "One of these days, someone's gonna to take you down a notch."

"Won't be you."

"Don't count on that," Wilf said under his breath.

Thorn turned the horse and rode toward the soldiers. There were only two, and they rode hard. Something was wrong. Out here in Indian country, unless they were scouts, soldiers traveled in large groups. Thorn waved, showing his empty hands.

Before Thorn could ask, the sergeant pulled his hard-used, drawn, and weary mount to a walk. "We got hit hard. Indians. Lost twelve men and our supplies." The gaunt, hollow-eyed soldiers looked worse than their horses. "It's bad. We've got to get to Fort Russell."

"When did you get hit?" Thorn asked, needing to know the proximity of the threat.

"Two days. We've got to get you and your men to Cheyenne. We can't protect you out here."

"I've got cattle."

"Leave them," the sergeant said as they rode over the hill and caught sight of the herd. "Where's the rest? Where's your remuda? We'll need horses."

"This is it," Thorn said.

As they rode up, Herb blurted out, "Where's the rest of your company?"

"Gone. All killed. Arapaho," the sergeant said. His shoulders slumped even lower and his head hung.

"What we going to do with you four?"

"We'll join up," Wilf said, taking charge. "We're stronger together. We'll leave these stinking cattle and force march to Cheyenne."

"Fourteen soldiers weren't enough. They're murdering and scalping everyone, even little babies," the sergeant said, "and burning every ranch along the front range. We've been riding hard for two days. We've got to get back to Fort Russell and muster all the troops."

"You men and your horses are worn out," Wilf said. "Our best bet is for Herb and me to take Thorn's horses and high tail it to the fort. We'll let the troops know what's happening, then get help and come back for y'all."

Thorn saw tension and worry in Wilf's face. He looked more afraid than heroic. What Wilf said had merit. The best tactic was to mount fresh men on the freshest horses and get help as soon as possible. He, himself, would be the wisest choice. He was the youngest, the strongest, and the best warrior. Above all, he needed to get Elly to safety. He owed her that and he wouldn't send her with Wilf and Herb.

Seeing the despair in the soldiers' eyes, he didn't trust them to protect Elly. "Elly and I, and one of you two should take all the horses and go," Thorn said to the soldiers.

"Why you?" Herb, asked.

"I'm younger and stronger, and I can ride day and night, and the horses are mine," Thorn replied, trying to find as many reasons as he could.

"And leave us here with no horses?" Wilf said. "You're just trying to save your own skin. You're yellow."

"My horses are fresh, and they'll make the trip without stopping. Elly's light and she can switch from one of your horses to the other," Thorn said to the Sergeant. "You've got to protect the woman."

The private spoke up, "I don't want to stay out here, Sergeant. You saw what those injuns done." The sergeant sat erect. "It's all right Jackson. This is a military responsibility. Jackson and I will take your horses."

"Take the girl, then," Thorn said.

"It's decided," the sergeant said, pulling back his shoulders like he was on the parade square. "Jackson and I will go on. We owe it to the men we lost. Our horses are done. They won't finish the kind of trip we need to make, even with the girl riding. There's still lots of other women out there that need help."

In desperation, Thorn thought of drawing his gun and taking Elly and his horses and making a run to Fort Russell, but Elly wasn't a fighter, and the sergeant was right about the cavalry mounts. They wouldn't make the forced ride. He didn't want to leave his cattle and he wouldn't leave Elly. "All right," he said. "Let's get these saddles switched over."

As the soldiers prepared to leave, Elly handed them a sack containing the remaining jerky and hardtack, food the soldiers could eat in the saddle. Thorn stroked the buckskin's neck. "He's a good one, the best I ever owned. He'll give you everything he's got."

"You'll find him at Fort Russell," the sergeant said. "We'll ride straight through and send help. God be with you." And they galloped away.

# Chapter 8

After the soldiers left, Thorn scouted, leaving Elly, Herb, and Wilf to keep the cattle moving. He kept them to low ground, following the flow of the land, taking more time to cover miles, but staying out of sight as much as possible. The worn-out horses took turns carrying the pack saddle and Thorn's saddle, but no one rode.

The men, and even Elly, marched with rifles in hand. Thorn insisted that every few minutes one of them check behind. With no way to hide or disguise their back-trail, he feared the Indians would ride across it and find them.

Except for the threat of Indian attack, life on the trail improved. They emerged from the path of the locust and, once again, there was grass for the cattle and horses. The sun shone and a light breeze cooled them and kept the bugs at bay. The area teamed with creatures escaping the devastation left by the locust. Herds of pronghorns grazed on every side. Mule deer browsed in every brush patch. Song birds sang and grouse flapped away at their passing.

Herb spotted a pack of wolves in the distance. Thorn worried they might be interested in his cattle, but decided that, with all the game concentrated in the area, they would steer clear of the cattle and the human scent around them.

As the day grew late, the breeze stopped. The air grew heavy and moist. Billowing thunderheads rose high above the western horizon. Sweat beaded, then dripped from their faces.

Scouting ahead, Thorn found a small creek in a deep wash. On the far side a treed bench of land, spread out against a rocky outcrop. He rode back. "It's early, but with that big storm heading our way. We'll hole up for the night."

After letting the cattle drink, they drove them onto the bench, above the tangled driftwood and clay banks that marked former high water. The cattle scratched on the trees and settled to grazing.

Against the bank, a huge rock outcrop provided shelter from any rain that may come. A rock circle and charred wood revealed they weren't the first humans to take shelter here. Wind and rain had stripped most of the black from the wood. It had been a long time since anyone used this fire ring.

Thunder rumbled in the distance. The creek

flowed faster, and the water grew cloudy as the storm drew near. The stream rose higher and higher. To the north and west, all vegetation striped away by the locust, nothing slowed the rainwater. It rushed into the swales and gullies, then gushed into the creek.

As the thunder grew louder, the creek roared. Muddier and deeper, it carried bigger branches and more debris.

"Are we safe here?" Elly asked Thorn.

"We're as safe as we've been in a while. We're well above the high water line. Even the Indians will keep their heads down in this storm. Let's build a fire and finish up the bacon and make some biscuits."

"That's right," Herb said, as he and Wilf gathered downed branches and broke them into smaller chunks.

Soon the smell of frying bacon and baking biscuits filled the air. Thorn had stretched his tarp on the windward side of the overhang, creating a warm cozy, shelter. As the storm blew closer, the thunder grew louder, the wind picked up, and the creek rose higher.

Wilf pulled his harmonica from the pocket of his sheepskin and played Dixie. Then he played Buffalo Gals. Herb sang along with the howling wind. For the first time since the locusts came, the four travelers relaxed.

As the storm passed overhead, the thunder crashed and crackled until had to cover their ears. The horses milled around and tugged at their pickets. The cattle snorted with fear. Over and over and over lightning streaked on every side, illuminating the night sky.

With a huge crash and a flash of fire, smoke, and shattering wood, a bolt of lightning struck an old cottonwood near the cattle. As one the cattle leaped up and stampeded down the valley. Thorn scrambled from under his bedroll and sprinted after them, Elly close behind.

Just around the bend, water rushing against a rock face blocked the stampede. As the cattle pushed forward, frantically trying to escape the lightning and fire, the bull slipped and fell into the torrent. Though he swam with great strength, the flood swept him downstream.

Thorn pushed past Elly and sprinted back to the horses. He could not afford to lose that bull. One or two cows would hurt his operation but losing the bull would be catastrophic. He'd been a fool to come all this way, with only one bull. If he lost him, the only place he knew to replace him, was all the way back in Eastern Kansas. He threw his saddle onto the sergeant's black gelding, cinched it tight and galloped up the wash, until he found a way around the rock and onto the hilltop.

He hustled the black as much as he dared in the dim light. Topping a rise well downstream, he saw the bull swimming, his massive shoulders driving him forward, until he found footing and scrambled from the water on the far side of the flood. Thorn, relief washing over him, relaxed in the saddle.

By now, the storm was moving beyond them, eastward. As Thorn rode back to camp, Elly ran to his side. "Did you see him?"

"Wouldn't survive that," Wilf said.

"He got across," Thorn replied. "I'm going to bring the cows back up here. He'll have to stay over there 'til the water goes down."

As Thorn brought the cows up near the camp, the

bull appeared across the wash, bawling, shaking his head, running up to the water's edge, then retreating, running up stream and then back down. The cows bawled back and moved to the edge of the flood.

The water was still rising as the prairie drained. The deluge was eighty feet wide in front of the camp and had risen twenty feet up the bank. Huge old driftwood trees, left high and dry by previous floods, bobbed along in the dirty foam.

Suddenly the bull rushed upstream, plunged into the water and swam desperately toward his herd. The water drove him downstream as he churned to get across.

Still mounted and not wanting to risk losing the bull, Thorn shook out his rope and threw it over the bull's massive head as he floated by. He took a dally around the saddle horn and tried to swing the big animal to the bank. The weight of the bull and the strength of the water pulled his horse toward the flood. The horse dug in. Thorn slid rope on the saddle horn until there was no more to give, then he threw a half hitch around the horn, unwilling to let the bull go.

The bull too heavy and the water too strong, the torrent sucked in Thorn and his horse.

Elly, Wilf, and Herb watched as bull, man, and horse disappeared around the bend. "Come on," Elly shouted, jumping to her feet and leading the way up and over the outcrop. She scrambled and grabbed handfuls of brush, rocks, and roots until she was at the top. Wilf and Herb followed.

She topped the rise in time to see Thorn and the horse on one side of an old cottonwood and the bull on the other. As the flood slammed against them, the rope tying them together pulled them under, as the water rushed against and over them.

As his head went under, Thorn cut the rope. He, the horse and the bull bobbed to the surface and raced down stream and over a tangled pile of driftwood. Thorn thrashed and tried to get over the debris, but his leather vest snagged on a branch. He was face up, but could not turn over or gain a hand or foothold on anything that would allow him to pull his body upstream and free himself. He twisted and turned and tried to find purchase for his feet or to kick against the current, but the water continued to pound against him and continued to rise.

Elly scrambled down the hill to the bank. Herb and Wilf followed. "He's stuck. Save him!" she shouted. "Save him!"

"I can't swim," said Herb.

Elly started for the torrent. Wilf grabbed her collar. "He's a gonner," he said, as Thorn's head disappeared under the water, arms and legs still flailing above the surface.

Thorn thrust up his face but could no longer get his nose above the flood. His lungs burned. He would keep fighting. A warrior never gives up. He finally had a reason to live. He had to save Elly.

Elly ripped free of Wilf's grasp and scrambled on hands and knees out onto the sweeper. She grabbed Thorn's hand. He jerked, almost pulling her in. She leaned against his pull. Still clinging to his hand, she fell into the water above the log that held him.

Close to blacking out, Thorn jerked on the hands that had grabbed him and forced himself against the current far enough to free his vest. Elly clung to his arm, struggling to hold them on to the log. The relentless, raging water washed her over the pile and swept them both downstream. Together they fought the current trying to reach shore. Thorn got a hand on a root and tried to cling to Elly as she swept by. His hand slipped, and she disappeared under the dirty foam.

He pulled himself up the bank and lay gasping. He reached deep and found the strength to rise and rush downstream. Running. Searching. He found her sprawled on the bank, unmoving. He sprinted to her, fell to his knees, and rolled her face up. Her chest rose, up and down, then she opened her eyes and smiled.

He cradled her head in his lap. "You're all right. It's all right. You saved me… and yourself. You're a warrior." It was the highest compliment he knew.

Once Elly was wrapped in her bedroll, Thorn searched the rest of the night for the horse and his bull. Finding neither, he staggered back into camp, soaked and shivering. Though the night was not cold, exhaustion, and disappointment left his body on the brink. He pulled off his soggy boots and dragged his bedroll over himself, without crawling in. A few minutes later, he heard Elly stir and tiptoe to his side. "Your teeth are chattering," she whispered, as she smoothed her blanket over his.

"I'll be alright," he said. "I'm just worn out. You saved me back there. I owe you my life."

"You'd have done the same," she said, as she crawled under the blankets and pressed herself against his back, wrapping him in her warmth.

He had no right to her warmth. Once she found out who he was, she would want nothing to do with him, but tonight he couldn't bring himself to push her away. As he lay there thinking of Breedlin, he wondered if Elly could ever forgive him or if he could ever forgive himself. He loathed the idea of telling her, but he knew he must, and sooner rather than later.

# Chapter 9

At first light, Thorn awoke to a distant high-pitched bawl. He crawled from the warmth and comfort of Elly and the blankets.

"What is it?" Elly asked, as he pulled on soggy boots.

"Sounds like my bull." Thorn smiled, as he headed to high ground. Before he got twenty strides, the bull trotted around the corner bellowing. The creek still carried a heavy load of mud and debris, but it had receded to no more that than three times its pre-storm flow. Once the big bull spotted the cows, he waded through the muddy water and joined them grazing on the wet grass. The lightning-struck cottonwood smoldered in the valley below, sending white smoke across the bright blue sky.

Thorn grabbed his rifle and set out to look for the horse. A mile and a half downstream, he found him, tangled in a mass of drift wood, well above the morning water line, but drowned. He worked his saddle free and for the second time, cut strips of meat from a horse.

When he carried his saddle back into camp, Wilf and Herb were at the top of the valley, heads together, murmuring. Each carried his rifle. Elly cooked biscuits, using the last of the coals from last night's fire and some bacon grease. She looked up with worried eyes. "They're planning to leave the cattle and make a run for Cheyenne. They're afraid of the Indians and think, if any help was coming from Fort Russell, we would have seen soldiers by now. Maybe we should all go get help and then come back for the cattle."

Thorn was furious. He had come so far and now they wanted to quit. "We're only two or three days out, four at the most," Thorn replied, more harshly than Elly deserved. "We'll be coming onto farms and ranches any day. I almost lost my bull once and I can't leave these Herefords. Not with a pack of wolves around. They're not fighters. Not like longhorns. They're all I have."

Elly stared into the pan of biscuits. "They're determined to leave the cattle and they're insisting I go with them. They said if you won't go, they'll just leave you with your cows and nothing else. I'm afraid now. I don't want to go with them. Not, without you."

She was right, he could not and would not let her

go alone with them.

Herb and Wilf started down the hill. "Morning boy," Wilf said heartily, limping down the hill. "Any luck with the horse?"

"Drowned."

"Sorry to hear that," Wilf said. "We needed that horse. I'm getting foot sore and the hairs been standing up on my neck all morning."

"Always been a bad sign. A fellar should listen when Wilf's hair stands up," Herb said.

"We need to make a run for it," Wilf said.

Herb moved away from Wilf as they approached. Both rifles, while still aimed at the ground, were cocked and pointed in Thorn's general direction.

"Drop those rifles," Thorn said, pistol suddenly in hand. "Just ease the hammers down and set them on the ground. And your gun belts."

"We's jes coming to suggest we leave them cattle and hightail it to Cheyenne, stay away from them 'Rapahos," Herb said. "You saw them soldier boys. We all did. Them's bad Injuns."

"Drop the guns!"

Wilf glared at Elly. "Why you so unfriendly all the sudden? Whatever she told you, we just want to keep our hair."

"She didn't have to tell me anything. I saw your cocked rifles and the way you spread out coming down the hill. You boys are easy to read. Drop those guns now! I won't say it again."

They eased the hammers down. As they bent to set the rifles on the ground, Wilf hacked and coughed, trying to draw Thorn's eyes, as Herb swung his rifle back up. An old trick, Thorn had seen before.

His bullet smashed the stock of Herb's rifle,

tearing it from his hands. Before Wilf could cock and raise his own rifle, Thorn had moved, and Wilf found himself staring into the gaping black hole of Thorn's pistol barrel. He dropped the rifle and showed his hands.

Herb thrust his hand to his mouth, then spit blood and shouted, "You blew my finger off!"

"Lucky it wasn't your head," Thorn said, keeping his eyes on Wilf. "Drop those gun belts and your pig stickers too. Now! I should just kill you both right here."

Elly gasped and covered her mouth.

Had Thorn been slower with his pistol, Herb would have shot him. The wise choice was obvious. He should have done it the day he had found them walking across the prairie. He needed to kill these men. No matter what they had done since the war, they hadn't changed. They were still the lowest kind of coyote, and the world would be better without them.

Wilf looked defeated, "Don't say that. We'll never make Cheyenne if we don't stick together. I see you're good with that pistol, but if the Indians come, one man ain't going to be enough to keep the girl safe. Fourteen soldiers couldn't save themselves."

Thorn paused and thought. Wilf had a point. Though they had seen no sign of Indians, there was no way of knowing where they might be or if they might have to fight them. Despite all their faults, Wilf and Herb were excellent fighters, and the three of them, with Elly's help, stood a better chance of fighting off the Indians than did he alone.

Wilf saw Thorn's hesitation and spoke more forcefully, "We just want to make a run for it and keep the girl safe. Your cows just slow us down. Give us back our guns, we'll take the girl and the horse and make a run for it. Think. The girl will be safe in town, we'll be safe, and you can just sit tight and guard your cattle, not making any dust or tracks and before you can say Jack Robinson, the soldiers'll be here to promenade you into Cheyenne."

Thorn knew Elly would never be safe alone with the two men. He knew them and he'd seen them watching her, increasingly as the days passed, following her with hungry eyes.

Thorn gathered the weapons, keeping his pistol pointed at the men. "Our back-trail's clean after this rain. We're only three or four days out. We'll get there."

# Chapter 10

Thorn and Elly led the pack horse out in front of the herd. Thorn wore Wilf's pistol on his left hip and carried all the ammunition in makeshift canvas pouches slung over his shoulder. Elly wore Herb's pistol around her waist and carried Wilf's rifle. Wilf and Herb limped along behind the cattle, keeping them moving.

Thorn scouted ahead, but tried to keep Elly, the men, and the herd in sight at all times. Anytime he left her side, he insisted she keep the rifle in hand.

Between his scouting forays, Elly questioned

Thorn. He avoided talking about his past, but he told her of his dream to raise the best beef; his plan to start out raising bulls, then selling beef to the men building the Northern Pacific Railroad and, once the line was built, to ship cattle east on the trains.

She asked about his family and he told her that a fever had got them when he was ten.

"Oh my. So young. How did you survive?"

"A man took me in."

"Who? He must have been a good man."

"I'd better scout ahead," Thorn said. He was not ready for his past to come out, still afraid of where the truth would lead. Soon he would tell her. "Keep an eye on those two."

When he returned, Elly again asked about his family.

"I hardly remember them," he said. "It hurt so bad to remember, I think I blocked it all out."

Elly reached out and stroked his cheek. "What about the man who took you in?"

Thorn relented, careful not to reveal too much. "He needed a servant. Called me his valet. At first he worked me like a slave, but I took it and, with time, he treated me like a son. He taught me everything. He came from the Kingdom of Serbia. He fought for the French before he came to America. He was a mercenary, a real warrior and wanted me to be the same."

"Where is he now?"

"Dead. Before he died, he told me I was the only thing he left in this world, that he was proud of. I wish I could say the same about myself. In many ways, he was a bad man, but I'd likely be dead if not for him. We did bad things."

"What things?"

"It's better I don't say."

"Is that why you won't tell me your name?"

"It's one reason. Tell me more about you."

"Growing up in Breedlin…"

Thorn darkened. "I better check those cows," he said and strode away. He couldn't think about Breedlin or what it meant for him and Elly.

They pushed the cattle until twilight. Again, a storm crashed in from the west. Thorn and Elly kept watch, huddled under his tarp in a small patch of buckbrush on a high point near the herd, the rifles and pistols between them. Wilf and Herb shivered below.

"What's wrong?" Elly asked. "You're so quiet. Did I do something wrong?"

"It's not you. I've just got a lot on my mind. You should get some sleep."

"I'm not sleepy. You sleep. I'll watch. There won't be anything moving in this storm, anyway. I'll wake you in a few hours."

"I doubt I'll sleep but thank you. The only vermin likely to move tonight are bedded down below. Keep an eye on them." With that Thorn closed his eyes. It was several hours before he awoke with his head resting on her lap and her fingers running through his hair. The storm had passed, and the Milky Way lit the night sky, stars so bright and clear you could almost touch them.

"Everything's quiet, but I can't keep my eyes open," she said.

"Thanks. I'll take over."

Elly got up and went behind the brush and out of sight. When she returned, she crawled under the tarp from the other side, snuggled into Thorn, and went to sleep. Elly pressed against him felt right. He knew he had to tell her what they had done, and he prayed she could forgive him.

The next day, after a breakfast of cold horse meat, Thorn and Elly took the lead. He was nervous, afraid of what he must say and of how she would react. As the ground dried, the cattle kicked up dust, and the breeze carried it around Wilf and Herb.

At noon, they stopped to rest the cattle and let them graze. "Why can't we take point," Wilf asked?

"I reckon we can scout ahead as good as a couple of pups like you," Herb added. "We was in the army killin' rebs, when you were still wet behind the ears. We know how to scout."

Elly jerked up her head and she and Wilf both glared at Herb, but no one said a word.

After a short break, Thorn and Elly took the drag.

The men out of earshot, Thorn turned to Elly. "My name is Thorn. Thorn Marshall."

"Thorn," she said, smiling. "Thorn Marshall. That's a good, strong name."

"I didn't tell you because I know these men and they know me. Or at least they knew me when I was a boy. You need to know who they are. If they get the chance or if anything happens to me, I'm afraid they'll hurt you. During the war, they served under the man who took me in. They haven't recognized me, but Wilf might be starting to figure it out. They're evil men."

"I've been so foolish."

"There's more," Thorn said.

Wilf held up an arm to stop them. Then waved Thorn ahead.

"Keep both hands on that rifle and don't be afraid to use it," Thorn whispered to Elly as he left.

"There's a flock of crows feeding up ahead. I don't see any other movement around them, but we should steer clear," Wilf said.

"Good work, Thorn said as he waived Elly forward. "If we follow this little swale east, it looks like we'll come out just below those crows and I can sneak up and have a look. You two take the drag."

"I reckon I don't like the smell of this. Give us our guns," Herb said.

"My hair's really standing on end now. I promise we won't cause you any grief," Wilf said.

"I'll hold 'em for now, but be ready."

"But Kansas," Herb whined.

"Come on Elly." Thorn started down the swale, leaving no time for argument.

At the end of the swale, Thorn crawled to the rim. After peaking over, he waved the others forward. A hundred yards to the west, the crows fed on the bodies of the two soldiers and what was left of Thorn's pack horse. A bald eagle swooped in and landed on one of the soldiers, scattering the crows.

"The Indians took meat from that horse. They're long gone. I can see tracks heading west," Thorn said. "We can't leave these men."

"I reckon we have to," Herb said. "Let's get as far from here as we can. Them Injuns are close."

"Give us our guns," Wilf argued, "and let's get out a here."

"I'm not leaving them," Thorn said, as he dropped his saddle from the top of the pack saddle and replaced it with all the guns except one pistol he left with Elly.

"Don't let them get close to you," he whispered. "I won't be far, and I won't be long."

\*\*\*\*\*

On a ridge, miles west, a sharp-eyed young warrior crawled into a patch of buckbrush to check the back trail. A fresh scalp hung from his waist. The war party of twelve was now ten young braves after coming onto the blue coat soldiers. He didn't want to lose any more men before they joined with the main group driving the settlers from their hunting grounds. A lone man and a horse, mere specks in the distance, appeared right where they had left the soldiers.

He despised every white man. Life was not easy before the white man came, but since, with each passing day, everything he knew slipped further and further away. And every day, more white men came.

He watched until the man and horse disappeared over the hill, then crouched deeper and crawled back to the other young braves.

\*\*\*\*\*

"Look away. You don't want to see this," Thorn warned Elly, as he dragged the men over the bank. The soldiers had bloody gunshot wounds and arrows poking out of their chests. Flies swarmed, buzzing around the ragged raw flesh where their hair had been. The private's skull was smashed in and tiny fresh-hatched maggots fed on his grayish pink brain. The sergeant stared, sightless, toward the sun. Thorn squeezed the eyelids over dull dry eyes.

Elly gagged at the stench of blood, rotting flesh, and excrement, but she gathered herself and picked up rocks to help cover the dead men. "Just watch them," Thorn whispered, once Wilf and Herb moved away to keep watch. "They're getting twitchy."

His sliced his tarp in two and rolled it around the soldiers, then he and Elly laid them in a shallow depression on the hillside and covered them with rocks and brush. "I wish I could do better for you men," he said, as he turned away and started the herd down the swale. He supposed there were people who loved the two soldiers, and he felt sorry that they were dead, but he thanked the Lord that they had refused to take Elly with them.

There would be no soldiers and no help. It was on him. Once they were safe, he would tell Elly about Breedlin. Right now, there were too many other things to do.

# Chapter 11

They pushed hard for the rest of the day. Thorn wanted to get far away from the battle site. As the sun set, he led them into a small shallow draw with steep banks on three sides. With no water, the horse and the cattle were restless. He dragged two dead trees across the open side and leaned as much brush as he could find against them. It wasn't enough to hold the animals if something spooked them, but maybe enough to keep them from wandering, if everything stayed quiet.

"I don't like this," Wilf said. "Give us them guns.

The hairs standing up on the back of my neck." "I reckon we'll need them guns 'fore the night's out," Herb said.

Thorn felt the danger in the air, but the pony tracks stretched west as far as he could see.

"I'm more worried about you two, than any Indians," Thorn said, as he checked the loads of all the rifles and pistols. "We'll all keep watch and if trouble starts, your guns will be right here, ready."

Herb and Wilf took first watch. Thorn dozed a little, his pistol in hand. At midnight, he and Elly climbed to the rim of the draw. "Any movement?" Thorn asked.

"Nothing," Wilf replied, "but my hair's still standing. It's coming."

The cool night air became bearable as Elly slipped close and wrapped an arm around his shoulder. Though he loved the warmth of her, the smell of her, the feel of her, he sat stiff and silent. How could she ever forgive him?

Elly laid a hand on Thorn's. "Do you have to go so far north? You could stay around Cheyenne." "I'm not fit to live around good people," he said, more harshly than he intended. "Besides, I'm told all the land's claimed around Cheyenne. If I ever want a place of my own, I have to go north."

"You're a good man," she insisted, leaning harder against him. "Are there towns, stores, schools up there?"

She felt right, leaning against him, but he didn't soften. "Not much yet, but once the Northern Pacific gets built, people will come and there will be all those things. Go to sleep now. I'll wake you in a bit."

War cries shattered the still dawn as ten young warriors thundered in.

"Get these guns to the men! Watch the cattle!" Thorn shouted, as he pushed Elly down the hill and turned and fired. A young warrior tumbled from his horse. He fired twice more, hitting a second warrior. The braves veered away. Bullets and arrows splattered around him, forcing him to duck below the small rock berm he had stacked in the night.

Behind him, Wilf and Herb began shooting.

Thorn jumped to his feet and sprinted for better cover over the edge of the hill. As he ran, a young brave wheeled his horse around and rode at him. Thorn slowed, but kept running, raised his rifle and shot the young man.

Another warrior galloped in from the side, pointing his lance at Thorn's chest. Thorn raise his rifle and pulled the trigger. Click! The rifle jammed! As fast as his pistol came out, the Indian was on him before he could bring it to bear. The lance inches from his chest, Thorn screamed his own war cry. He pivoted back and in toward the horse, blading his body, making the target as small as possible. The lance brushed his chest, doing no damage, but it caught on the cylinder of his pistol and tore it from his hand. As he pivoted into the horse, he grabbed the rawhide war bridle with his left hand, driving the horse's head into the dirt, causing it to somersault, slamming the young warrior to the ground and jerking Thorn from his feet. Before the brave could pull his broken lance from the earth, Thorn was up, knife in hand.

"THORN!" Elly screamed from the mouth of the little valley where she had been struggling to keep the cattle contained. A strong, tall brave, on a large sorrel horse, was dragging her away by her hair.

Thorn glanced toward Elly as the young brave charged. If not for the hours spent fencing and training with sabers, the splintered end of the lance would have impaled him. Instead, he moved just enough that the splintered shards of wood only caught his shirt. As the young brave skidded to a stop, Thorn feinted with his left hand, stepped in, knife edge up, and opened him from navel to heart, jamming his knife deep into the bone of his spine.

Head shaking, the Indian pony struggled to its feet. Thorn pulled at his knife, but his hand slipped off the blood-slicked handle. Elly! There was no time. He left the knife, leaped onto pony's back and kicked wildly. The horse stumbled a few steps, then gathered itself and lunged toward Elly, who thrashed and clawed at the big Indian trying to take her.

The brave raised his rifle for a shot at Thorn. Elly jerked down and nearly dragged him off the horse. He smashed the rifle butt into her head, and she slumped. The brave dropped Elly and raised the rifle again, but before he could to get a shot off, Thorn drove his fear-crazed mount into the side of the brave's horse, crashing men and horses to the ground and knocking the rifle from the warrior's hand.

Both men rolled free of the scrambling horses and came to their feet. Before Thorn could get to the rifle, the brave whipped out his knife and charged. Thorn stumbled but turned enough to avoid the blade as the warrior rushed by and beyond him. Shuffling the knife from hand to hand, the warrior tested the unarmed Thorn. He feinted with the left. Thorn stepped back easily. The warrior thrust again, the knife in his right hand. They circled one another, looking for any opening, eyes locked together. The brave feigned with the left and switched hands and thrust with the right, catching Thorn and leaving a shallow gash in his side.

The brave smiled. Thorn nodded and smiled back.

In the background, Thorn heard rifle shots, but held his eyes locked on the fighter in front of him.

The brave passed the knife from one hand to the other. He feinted with the left, then the right—then left. Each time, Thorn stepped aside easily. Again, the young warrior thrust with the left, passed the knife into his right hand and thrust further and deeper to the right. Thorn leaned away from the left-hand thrust, then stepped into the brave, grabbed his right arm with both hands and pulled him into a hard knee strike. Then he rotated his hips bringing them both crashing to the ground.

The knife fell free and the two men thrashed and grappled for advantage. The big fighter was shirtless and slippery. Each time Thorn got a good hold, the warrior bit, clawed, and scrambled, until he broke free. Thorn battled, never losing contact. Each time the warrior broke a hold, Thorn struck and repositioned, until he found the position he knew would bring him victory. He straddled the brave's back and locked his left arm around the sweaty neck, cupping the back of the slippery warrior's head with his right. He squeezed with everything he had. The brave thrashed, twisting his head and his whole body first left, then right, left, right. He pushed hard with his legs and ended on his back with Thorn below him, but Thorn held tight. The warrior arched his back and clawed streaks in Thorn's arms. They rolled over the rocky ground, but Thorn held on until the fighter went limp and then he held on longer, squeezing ever harder. His arms burned and trembled with the effort.

From somewhere far away, he heard a voice, Elly's voice. "He's dead Thorn. He's dead. You can let go." She caressed his shoulder until he relaxed his bleeding arms and slumped back on his haunches.

The gunfire stopped.

A bloody auburn scalp hung from the rawhide belt around the warrior's waist. The private.

Two young braves galloped west, leaving eight more brothers in arms unmoving on the brown prairie grass.

# Chapter 12

Elly dropped the Indian's rifle and cupped Thorn's face in her hands. "I'd tried to shoot him," she said, "but you were too close. Are you all right?"

"I'm fine," he said, melting into her touch.

"Isn't that cute," Wilf said, as he strolled up, his rifle aimed at Thorn. "See the hammer back on this rifle now?"

"I reckon it's the cutest thing I ever seen," Herb replied. "Little Prick and the princess all lovey dovey." Thorn bristled at the old nickname.

"Thought we wouldn't figure it out, didn't you Little Prick," Wilf said. "I had me a suspicion, but when I looked up and saw you slip that lance and heard that war cry, I knew. You sound just like the Colonel. He'd be proud of you. The son he never had."

Herb grinned. "I reckon the girl sealed it when she called out your name. I'm hurt, you'd tell her but not your ol' friends who you were."

Thorn laughed but his eyes remained cold. "We were never friends."

"Ouch. That hurt." Wilf smiled. "Now get on your belly and put your hands behind your back old friend and don't try anything stupid. It seems after you got us kicked out, the Colonel taught you a thing or two, so just do as you're told, or we'll shoot the girl."

Herb set his rifle on the grass and tried to tie Thorn's hands behind his back with a section of the driving rein, Thorn had taken from the team. His bandaged finger made it difficult to make a good tie.

"Let me," Wilf said. "We don't want him getting away." Thorn's eyes scanned left and right.

"Keep your rifle on the girl." Wilf said. "Behave yourself boy." He knelt and tied Thorn's hands. Then he stood up and kicked Thorn in the face.

Elly gasped.

Wilf chuckled, as he tied Elly's hands. "That'll teach him not to keep secrets from his friends."

Once Elly was tied, Herb walked over and caressed her cheek and neck. She flinched and pulled away. "This filly's still a little wild," he said. "I reckon I'm gonna enjoy breakin' her."

"In good time," Wilf said. "We need to get

moving. By sunset, I want to be far from here and these stinkin' cattle. Once we get close enough to civilization, that them young bucks won't try to sneak back in on us, we'll take good care of these two."

As they walked, Herb tripped Elly, who flopped to the ground, unable to break her fall, her hands tied behind her back. "Clumsy," Herb laughed.

"Leave her alone," Thorn warned.

"I'm sacking her out, getting' her used to being touched, just like a little wild pony," Herb said, as he reached around and grabbed her by the breasts and pulled her to her feet. Thorn lunged, driving his head into Herb's midsection and knocking him to the ground with a thump. Wilf kicked Thorn in the back of the legs, knocking him onto his face. Both men kicked him again and again.

Thorn rolled into a ball and tucked his chin to protect himself, but one sharp kick landed with a crack. It felt like a broken rib.

"Stop," Elly begged. "You'll kill him."

"We aim to," Wilf said, "but you're right, we don't want to bust him up too much yet. We might need him before we get to civilization. One of us'll just hold a rifle in your ear and let him take care of the savages. He's as good as I've ever seen. The old Colonel taught him well."

Hands behind his back, Thorn stumbled along, the broken rib flashing pain with every step and every breath.

That night they made camp in a grove of cottonwoods on a clear, clean creek. Before dropping into the valley, they'd seen lights far to the south, probably a ranch house.

They tied Thorn and Elly on either side of a small poplar, using the last of the bridle rein to lash them together.

They unsaddled the pack horse, threw the saddle in a heap, and started a fire. Herb left to keep watch while Wilf dug out the remains of the food and mixed up the last of the flour for biscuits. Once the biscuits were ready, Herb came to the fire.

"Slim pickins tonight," Wilf said.

"Maybe not," said Herb, pointing to the pack saddle. A porcupine chewed on the salty latigos. Herb picked up a long stick and tiptoed over to the round creature. The porcupine bristled and blew up to twice his size. He turned his rear toward Herb and thrashed his spiny tail. Herb flicked him over with the stick and speared the soft underbelly with the sharp branch. The porcupine jerked and flopped on the stick, then relaxed and died.

Before long, porcupine meat sizzled in the frying pan. "Not bad," said Herb, "other than the bark taste." He grabbed a sizzling strip between two fingers and offered it to Elly. She turned her head. "Eat it" he said. "We need to put some meat on your bones." He grabbed her jaw and turned her face toward him, trying to force the meat into her mouth. She clenched her teeth. Herb laughed and ate the meat himself. "You'll get hungry enough 'for we're done." Then he wiped his hands on her body. Elly glared, but didn't move. "See Wilf, she's already starting to like it." Elly spit in his face. Herb grabbed her jaw and kissed her hard on the mouth. She bit his lip, drawing blood. He slapped her, knocking her head against the tree.

"Leave her alone," Thorn warned, struggling against his ties.

"Settle down boy," Herb said. "You ain't long for this world and I reckon we got big plans for your little lady friend here. We're still gonna be pards, only not in the freight business. We're going into the whorin' business."

"Never!" Elly said, fire flashing from her eyes.

"It's an honorable profession," Wilf said. "Some say it's the world's oldest, though I'm thinking farming is older, or maybe even preaching or robbing, but never the less, even the good Lord Jesus loved Mary Magdalene."

"You can't force me. I'll get away. I'll go to the law and they'll hang you both."

"You do that and, since we'll be dead men anyway, before the law gets us, we'll get to your aunt and uncle and make 'em watch while we kill your little niece and then we'll kill them. Ask your beau. He knows we'll do it." Wilf grinned. "We weren't just Sunday strolling back there behind those stinking cows. We've thought this through."

Elly shrunk into herself, hopeless. Hopelessness swept over Thorn as well, but he fought it back. Yes, the Colonel had taught him to fight, but he also taught him, that no matter how dark, how desperate, how hopeless a situation, a true warrior keeps his head, until he finds a way to survive. A warrior never gives up and a warrior would never leave a woman to these two.

After supper, Wilf took the watch. Two hours later, he returned and sent Herb up the hill. "I can't believe I took this long to recognize you Little Prick, I should've seen that scar running up to your eye. I remember that day in Breedlin when the Colonel gave you that little reminder. That was a good day."

"Breedlin?" Elly gasped. "You never told me you were in Breedlin." Thorn slumped. Now she knew.

"Yeah, we thought we should keep that little secret too," Wilf laughed. "Young Thorn was with us the day we liberated Breedlin. Guess we should have told you sooner, but when we met you, we were keeping our previous visit a secret and it somehow seemed better to leave it that way."

*****

Elly remembered the day her father died. The young men had already left Breedlin for the army. From the beginning, most from Missouri sided with the south and many of those that didn't, changed their minds once the Red Legs swept in from Kansas, killing and robbing, in the name of the Union.

The Raiders galloped into town in the middle of the day, guns drawn and faces masked, like the common bandits they were. The men left in the village grabbed guns and tried to fight the raiders off.

Hearing the gunfire, Elly's father rushed her to the back of the store. "Run!" he said. "Hide in the corn. Don't come out 'til they're gone."

She had just started across the open ground between the store and the fields when two masked raiders galloped in from the far end of the street. She ducked between her father's store and the hotel. She could hear the raiders behind the store yelling orders, calling on the townspeople to surrender. Out front, raiders galloped up and down the street firing into the buildings. She was trapped.

She peeked out from between the buildings. The raiders had moved further down, toward the back of the livery. She ached to run for the safety of the corn. She knew she could hide there. She had hidden there many times playing games with her brother and their friends. She started, then ducked back between the buildings, when the raiders wheeled their horses back toward her.

Had they seen her? She ran toward the street, then back toward the corn, nowhere safe to go. She saw her father's big freight wagon parked near the street. She could hide there. She sprinted to it, hoping the raiders hadn't seen her. She dove up, scrambled over the end gate and crawled under the heavy canvas tarp stored under the seat.

Through the slats of the wagon box, she saw raiders galloping up and down the street, firing into the buildings. She heard a shotgun blast, and a raider threw up his hands and tumbled from his horse. She knew her father had shot the beast. She felt proud. He and the other men would protect her and drive the Red Legs away.

A bugle sounded, and the raiders were gone. They'd won. Her father had driven the evil men away. She sobbed with relief and started to crawl out from under the tarp when she heard women wailing and crying.

A man shouted in a strange accent. "Good men of Breedlin, Missouri drop your weapons and come out into the street."

"Never," Old Mac Brooks, shouted from the livery.

Elly crawled back under the tarp and choked back her sobs.

"Your choice," the man shouted, but we've got five lovely ladies here that will never see another sunset unless you do exactly as I tell you. Everyone. Out in the street. Now! Hands where we can see them. The first woman dies in ten seconds. One…. Two…."

The men filed into the street and were marched to the front of the hotel. "On your knees," the man shouted. "We've come to liberate your lovely village…" Some of the masked men laughed. "…from the tyrannical grip of the evil slave-holding Confederacy. And we've come to exact a tax, for the good of the glorious Union."

Just give them what they want, she thought, and let them go away. Her heart raced and her hands were cold and clammy

"But alas first we must seek justice for the cold-blooded criminal murder of our comrade-in-arms." Elly barely breathed as she watched her father and the other men kneeling in the street. The man who had been shouting orders, walked into her view and stopped behind the kneeling men. He stood straight, tall and slim. He wore a clean, long uniform coat, with gold fringe on the shoulders, a saber on one hip, a pistol on the other. Below the knees of his dark blue breeches, he wore fringed red leather leggings.

"Who killed my comrade?" he asked loudly in his European accented voice. "Come now. If no one confesses, you will force me to execute you all."

Elly's father raised himself. "I did it. Let the rest go."

"Father no," she whispered, her entire body

quivering.

The tall raider laughed. "A brave man and I'm certain that your sacrifice will be rewarded in the great beyond, but as an officer of the glorious Union, I cannot accommodate your request. It falls to me to deter other enemies in other towns from killing our liberators. As such, I am obligated, even duty bound, to exact a toll of five men to one. Boy, come."

A slight young man, with blonde, almost white, hair showing under his hat and over his mask, came forward.

"Today you become a man. Take out your pistol."

"I don't want to do it, sir."

"Take out your pistol!"

The young man pulled an old pistol from his holster.

"This is no different from killing a rabid dog or a horse with a broken leg. It is an unpleasantness that, as a man, one must take on. Start with this one," the man said, pointing at Elly's father.

"I can't do it, sir. I won't."

"You must!" the man roared. The boy pointed the pistol at her father's head.

Elly bit her own arm to keep from screaming and squeezed her eyes tightly closed. Six shots rang out. The women at the end of the street screamed and wept. When Elly looked up, her father and five other men, five good friends and neighbors, lay dead in the dusty street.

\*\*\*\*\*

"You were the boy," Elly sobbed. "You killed

him."

"I was there," Thorn whispered, "but I didn't kill your Pa."

"I saw you!" Elly screamed, tears streaming down her red cheeks.

Herb leaped up and slapped Elly's face. "Quiet whore, you'll bring the whole Indian nation down on us."

"Leave her alone," Thorn said, defeated. How had he let this happen? He had underestimated Wilf and Herb, and now his cattle were wolf bait and the woman he....? What did he feel for her? It didn't matter. He'd failed her and even if he hadn't, she would never forgive him. He'd been overconfident and let his feelings for her distract him. He was no warrior and now they would both pay.

# Chapter 13

Deep in the night, Herb paced around the smoldering remains of the fire. He shook Thorn awake with his boot. "Hey wake up. I cain't sleep. Tomorra, we're gonna break that girl in, an you're gonna watch. The last thing you'll ever see is my ass on your girl. Life was good with the Colonel, pretty much all a man could ask for. Had to do a little fightin', but that came with its pleasures. Most the time, we was jes setting 'round while the Colonel scouted and planned, but you had to go and ruin it. Tomorra's gonna be a good day."

Thorn had nothing to say. He had let his feelings for Elly get in the way of protecting her and had failed her and failed himself. He deserved whatever happened.

Herb laughed. "We're gonna be living in the land of milk and honey. After all these years and all the hard times, we've found our callin'."

"Go to Hell," Thorn rasped out.

"Oh no," Herb grinned. "I got that one figured out too. Actually, Wilf figured it out. I must a heard him preach that sermon fifty times. It says right in the good book, that all a fella's gotta do is confess the Lord Jesus and believe in his heart that God raised him up from the dead, and he'll be saved. People like to hear that. That sermon made us some good money. The Good Book says I can just do whatever it is I want, jes' as long as, right before I close my eyes for the last time, I tell the Good Lord I'm sorry and tell Him I believe. I'm sure 'nough gonna do that and I'm sure 'nough gonna believe and the angels are sure 'nough gonna take me up."

"Things are finally going my way," Herb continued. "Take you. Who'd a ever thought the Good Lord would deliver you right here into my hands after all these years. I guess it's my reward for making all those folks happy with my singin'."

"Herb!" Wilf whispered, returning to camp. "Leave the boy alone. You're gonna need your strength. We got a filly to break. Make sure they're tied good. You and me are going to do a little reconnaissance. These two are gonna make some noise in the morning, so we've got to make sure there's no one around to surprise us."

"I can't hardly wait," Herb said, excitement in his voice.

After the men had been gone long enough to be well away from camp, Thorn whispered, "I was there, but I didn't kill them. I swear it."

"Don't lie!" she hissed. "You've lied enough. I was there too. I saw you. Don't talk to me." Just then, the rustling of leaves and the cracking of branches warned that the men returned. Thorn felt the ties binding them together gently jerking as Elly silently sobbed. He deserved whatever came, but he had to find a way to help the girl. He owed her that.

Thorn struggled against his ties until his wrists burned, then bled, then went numb. Finally, he rested, gathering his strength for another try. Just before dawn, Elly gasped. Herb snored rhythmically a few feet away.

"What's wrong?" Thorn breathed.

"Look at the tree," she whispered.

Thorn twisted his head back and, from the corner of his eye, saw the outline of a porcupine climbing, tail first, from the tree they were tied to. Elly breathed heavily.

"Shhhh," Thorn hissed. Hold still.

The porcupine inched to the ground. As it crawled over, it sniffed at the salty bridle rein, tying them to the tree. Dropping its back feet to the ground, it licked the rein and then gnawed at the salt. Thorn and Elly both held their breath. Thorn waited until he thought the rein might be weak enough, then he slowly, quietly leaned against it. Pain shot from his raw wrists and up his arms to his neck. He bit his tongue to keep from crying out. The ties held. The porcupine bristled at the movement but stayed put and resumed chewing. Thorn waited and leaned again.

No give and more pain. He listened for Herb and Wilf. "This time, when I pull, you pull too. We've got to get free now! Twist!"

The rein broke, leaving them free of the tree and each other, though their hands remained tied behind their backs. The porcupine swelled and bristled, then dropped its front feet to the ground, turned and waddled away.

Thorn listened again. Herb snored near the fire and he could not hear Wilf, who was still somewhere on the hill above keeping watch. "See if you can untie my hands."

Elly hesitated. Thorn touched her forehead with his. "You need to get away. Do it for you."

They turned back to back and she started at the bloody knots with her fingertips "I can't get it. Try mine."

The old bridle reins were dry and raspy, and Thorn's hands had little feeling after being tied so long. Finally, he gave up and struggled and bent until he pulled his feet one at a time through his arms, getting his hands to his front. Elly, seeing him, did the same thing. He worked the knots with his teeth. "Let me," Elly said.

As she struggled with the knots, Thorn surveyed the campsite. His rifle leaned against a tree just beyond the snoring Herb and his pistol hung near it. The pack horse nibbled on something just beyond the firelight.

The crackle of branches breaking warned that Wilf was coming down the hill. Hands still tied, Thorn sprinted toward for his rifle. "What the hell!" Herb shouted tossing off his covers. Thorn, focused on the rifle, hit the flying blanket and tripped as Herb fired a shot from his pistol.

A brutal blow struck Thorn just above the belt on his left side. As he fell, he drove his knees into Herb's arm, knocking the pistol from his hand. Herb twisted and sprang onto Thorn's back.

Hearing the shot, Wilf bulled down the hill, rifle ready. Elly grabbed up the closest weapon she could find, a large, heavy branch. She swung at Wilf's head as he broke into the clearing. The branch was long and awkward, and Wilf saw motion, threw up the rifle and partially blocked the blow.

Herb pressed forward locking Thorn in a bear hug. Thorn threw back his head trying to break Herb's nose. Herb turned his face at the last second and took the blow on his cheek.

Wilf pointed the rifle at the swinger of the branch. Seeing Elly, he drove the rifle barrel into her midsection, knocking the wind out of her and driving her to the ground. "Stay there, whore!" he shouted.

Thorn rolled out from under Herb and struck a two-handed blow to the side of his head, stunning the smaller man. With the surge of energy brought on by the fight, Thorn forgot his pain and injuries.

As Thorn and Herb rolled apart, Wilf leveled his rifle. As he squeezed the trigger, Elly drove her shoulder into his back. The bullet smashed high into Herb's chest, knocking him back and away from Thorn. "You made me shoot Herb! Herb!" He swung his rifle viciously, knocking Elly back to the ground.

Thorn grabbed Herb's pistol, with two hands and pointed at Wilf. As Thorn shot, Elly dove at the rifle in Wilf's hands. Thorn's bullet struck her in the head, and she fell at Wilf's feet.

He'd killed her! His blood turned cold and his vision hyper-focused. Vengeance was all that remained.

As Wilf scrambled along the ground searching for cover. Thorn eared back the hammer and drew a bead. As he squeezed the trigger, Herb kicked him, then jumped on his back. The bullet tore through Wilf's bicep, knocking the rifle from his hands. Thorn bucked and scrambled, trying to dislodge Herb, while firing more wild shots, until the pistol clicked, empty. Wilf ducked and dodged through the trees, firing his pistol as he ran. He jumped bareback onto the last of the soldiers' horses and galloped away, crashing through trees and undergrowth, until he disappeared over the ridge.

Herb, not realizing how hard he was hit, tore at Thorn's shirt. Thorn spun and grabbed him around the throat. He squeezed as hard as he could. Herb bucked and pawed at Thorn's arms, but he had no strength and soon passed out. Thorn released him, then stumbled up the hill to Elly. She lay motionless in a heap, her beautiful hair, now blood soaked, spread across her face. Thorn dropped to his knees, fell back on his haunches and wept.

Elly moaned.

Thorn lurched forward and swept the hair from her face. Her eyes twitched, then fluttered opened and closed and open and closed again and finally opened. "What happened?" she asked.

"You saved me again," he said.

She looked into his eyes, then turned away.

At least she was alive, Thorn thought, as he pulled

the knife from Herb's belt and cut the ties around her wrists. Without meeting his eyes, she took the knife and cut him free. Thorn reached up to touch her head. She jerked away. "You're hit," he said. "I just want to make sure you're all right."

She reached up and felt the blood in her hair, then the shallow bullet crease in her scalp. Shock had numbed the pain. She held up her hair and allowed Thorn to examine the wound. He grabbed a small branch from the edge of the smoldering fire and blew on it until it flared. It looked like the bullet had grazed her, cutting a furrow in the skin, but missing the bone.

Thorn dug through his saddle bag, when Herb coughed and came too. He was hit hard and dying. "Lord Jesus, I believe, and I accept your grace," he cried. "I reckon I'm sorry for all the wickedness I done."

"Tell her what happened in Breedlin," Thorn said, as he pressed the knife to his throat. "Tell her who killed those men."

"I don't know, I reckon you did," Herb, said, chortling through the blood in his throat.

"You'll burn," Thorn warned, grabbing Herb's shirt and pulling his shoulders off the ground. "You've got this figured, but you can't die with a lie on your lips. Your time's short."

Herb coughed and cleared his throat, spitting blood. "He never killed 'em," he said. "He was too scared and weak. That's why the Colonel cut his face. When the boy hesitated, Wilf jes' walked up, nice as pie and shot 'em all. Even shot an extry. The Colonel didn't like that much, he wanted the boy to do it, but

Wilf weren't scared."

Elly slumped to her knees.

\*\*\*\*\*

Now she remembered. A good while after the shots, she'd come back to herself and peeked through the slats of the wagon. Her beloved father and the other dear men lay face down. Around each of their heads, a halo of blood blossomed out into the dust of the street. Before she'd torn her eyes away for a second time, she now remembered seeing the white-haired boy, standing defiant, eyes blazing, blood oozing from his cheek and dripping off the end of his chin. The tall man stood nearby holding an ornate calvary saber.

\*\*\*\*\*

Herb breathed rhythmically and smiled. "I see 'em coming. I see the angels coming. No!" he whispered. He stared wide-eyed at the sky. His face filled with fear as the only angels he would ever see came to take him home. "I told the truth. No… Sweet Jesus… Sweet Jesus," he cried. "Noooo!" he screamed as he fell back. A few ragged, bloody breaths bubbled past his lips and he died, fear etched on his face.

"Gone to where he belongs," Elly said.

Thorn swayed on shaking legs. The heat of the battle gone, his injuries took their toll. Elly noticed blood darkening his pant leg. "You're hit," she said. The bullet had torn through the right side of Thorn's belly and out the back.

"Leave it," Thorn said, feeling he had nothing left to live for. "I guess Herb's angels will be coming for me soon."

"Sit down! You'll not die on me now."

Thorn slumped to his knees. He struggled to hold on to consciousness. What had she said? 'You'll not die on ME now?' What did that mean?

She grabbed the pack saddle and Herb's blankets and laid him back against them. She cut the cleanest strips she could find from her petticoats, packed the holes, front and back, and used a strip of Herb's dirty shirt to bind them in place. Then she found the saddle bags, containing her most precious belongings, picked up a pistol and struggled to help Thorn to his feet. He dug deep and, with her help, pushed himself up.

The ranch, they had seen in the distance, was less than three miles away. As she half carried Thorn out of the creek bottom, riders rode in fast. Thorn's legs gave way, and she lowered him to the ground.

As the riders pulled up, rifles cocked and ready, the leader, a strong-jawed young man said, "We heard shooting. Indians?"

"No… Much worse," Elly answered.

# Chapter 14

When Thorn came back to himself, he smelled lavender. He opened his eyes and the first thing he saw, was Elly dozing in a big leather chair near the bed where he lay. He started to get up, until the pain reminded him of the beating and the gun shot. Pulling back the covers, he saw a clean bandage wrapped around his middle. Round, purple and yellow bruises dotted his belly and thighs.

Elly opened her eyes. "You're back." She smiled. She stood, took a cloth from a basin by the bed, and wiped his brow.

"I've got to go get my cattle," Thorn said, trying to rise.

Elly placed a hand on his shoulder and gently held him down. "The cattle are fine. They're here."

"All of them?"

"Yes sir," Elly smiled. Then she creased her eyes and furrowed her pretty brow as she reached out and caressed Thorn's cheek. "I'm sorry."

"What are you sorry for? You saved me."

I'm sorry I accused you. I'm sorry I doubted you."

Thorn looked away. "I don't deserve forgiveness. You have every right. I was there and I've hurt and killed enough people, that…"

A gentle knock on the door interrupted them. A tall dark-haired man pushed the door open a crack, then stepped in. "I thought I heard talking in here." He held out his hand. "Bob Pratt."

Thorn felt the strong grip as they shook. "Thorn Marshall. Pleased to meet you. Seems like I owe you many thanks."

"Not at all," Bob replied. At that moment, a kind-faced, blonde woman entered. "This is my wife."

"I'm Margaret," she said, holding out her hand. "I'm so happy to see you awake. I hope my boys didn't disturb you too much. We tried to keep them quiet or outside."

"I haven't heard a thing, until just now," Thorn replied. "Sorry to put you through all this bother."

"No bother to us," Margaret said. "Miss Elly here did most of it."

"Once we got you back here, and the Doc arrived, she wanted to lead a posse after that Wilf. I convinced her she'd do more good here nursing you, though that part didn't take much convincing," Bob smiled. "I couldn't talk her out of leading us out to bring in that herd of cattle of yours though. Since we got the cattle back safe, she's been here. Hardly left this room."

"I had to get Bob to bring up that old wing-back, or she'd a slept on the floor," Margaret said.

"We picked up your saddle and pack saddle too, though the porcupines chewed them up a fair bit," Bob said.

"Those little fellas are welcome to them, after what they did for us," Thorn said, then laughed, until he winced at the pain in his chest.

"You need to rest," Elly said, shooing Bob and Margaret from the room.

Over the next couple of days, Elly told Thorn what had happened. After Bob and his men found them, they brought him to the ranch house. Bob sent a man to Cheyenne to fetch the Doctor. After hearing Elly's story, Bob some of his men and some neighbors went out to find Wilf. Even with a wounded arm, Wilf proved wily prey, and they'd returned without him. They did find the bodies of the soldiers and had given them a proper burial.

They found the Herefords grazing along a small creek, not far from where they had last left them. They now grazed in a pasture near the house.

After three more days, Thorn awoke just as the sun started to stream into the room. He could hear Elly and Margaret talking quietly in the kitchen. He pulled off the blankets and dropped his feet to the floor. His side hurt and he saw there was still blood and yellow stains on the dressing, but he pushed himself up and shuffled to the window.

Not far from the house, his cattle grazed in a pasture along a little creek.

Elly walked in, gasped, and spun away, closing the door. Thorn realized he was naked except for the bandage around his waist. "Sorry about that," he said.

"It's alright," Elly said, with laughter in her voice, "but you should be in bed."

"I couldn't stay down another minute."

"There are clothes on the chair. If you're going to be up, I suppose you'd better get dressed. I'll come back."

Thorn found clean clothes, he assumed must belong to Bob. Once dressed, he dropped into the big leather chair.

"You can come in now," he said. "I'm so sorry. I just had to get up and see if I could see my cattle. I didn't even notice I was naked."

"It's all right," she replied, her pale cheeks reddening. "It's not like I haven't seen you…" Thorn looked at her. "Someone had to clean you up and bath you while you were out…." Now it was Thorn's turn to blush. "Once you feel up to going downstairs, I have a surprise for you," Elly said with a lilt in her voice. "A good surprise."

"I like good surprises. I suppose I could make it now, with a little help." "Before we go down, I've been wanting to trim your hair a little. I used to do it for my Daddy."

"I suppose I could use a little clip," Thorn smiled, as he turned and saw himself in the mirror. He was as thin as he could remember. With his hair and beard long and shaggy, he looked like a mountain man.

A few minutes later, Elly returned with soap,

scissors, a razor, and a bowl of hot water. She touched his beard. "Could I shave this off too?"

"Why not?"

First, she cut his hair. Then she clipped his beard short with the scissors.

"Lean back a little," she whispered.

Steam rose from the towel as she placed it against his skin. The warm water soothed and relaxed the muscles of his face as it softened his whiskers. He could smell a hint of mint as she lathered a bar of soap between her hands. Using just her hands, she smoothed the lather over his bristly cheeks and under his chin. As she scraped down his cheek, he could hear the sharp blade click through the stiff hairs.

He'd never enjoyed a shave more.

She wiped the razor, then taking a warm wet cloth, caressed his cheeks and throat, removing the remaining soap and whiskers. With a fresh towel, she gently dried his skin. As she finished, she ran her finger down the narrow, pale scar that ran from near his left eye to his jaw line, sending tingles down his spine.

Uncomfortable, almost overwhelmed, with the emotions he was feeling, he said, "Let's go see this surprise."

As they stepped on to the wide veranda, two cowboys sitting on large wooden chairs, saluted Thorn with large glasses of milk. Thorn laughed. "This is a surprise." Arlin and Rufus, two of the Texas cowboys he had met on the Oregon trail, stood and took turns shaking his hand.

A few days after meeting Thorn on the trail, the two Texans had ridden to Cheyenne and to see if they could find him or the herd he had mentioned. The more they talked and thought about Montana, the more it seemed they needed to get back there. Neither had anything nor anyone pressing back home in Texas, and that Montana country was a cattleman's dream. A man could make his own life up there.

"How'd you find me here?" Thorn asked, after greeting and shaking hands with the men.

Arlin shook his head and laughed. "It weren't hard. Mostly we just followed the crows and coyotes to the dead things."

"You do cut a swath," Rufus said, grinning.

Two days later, Thorn walked into the kitchen. Bob sat alone, nursing a cup of coffee. "I guess it's time for me to head north," Thorn said.

"You're welcome to stay on longer," Bob said. "I could use a good man this fall and winter. You could head north in the spring."

"You've done enough for a stranger already," Thorn said, "and I've got it in me to get started. If I wait any longer, it'll be too late to get set up this year."

"Yes, you're right," Bob said. "It's not my place to say, but Elly's a fine woman. She's one to ride the river with and well beyond."

"She is," Thorn said, "but I'm not."

"I'm a pretty good judge of a man and I think Elly is too, and we agree on you."

"You don't either one know all the things I've done."

"It's a hard, rough land out here, and we judge a man by what he does now, not what he done before he came, especially what he done as a boy."

"Thank you for the offer and the kind words Bob,

but I've got it in me to go," said Thorn. "Would you be willing to sell me a couple of good horses?"

"I will. In fact, I've been thinking about it since you got here, but before we go look, I won't beg, but I could shore use you this fall and winter." Thorn just shook his head.

"All right. The boys have a bunch in the corral. Come on out and take your pick." As they rounded the barn, Thorn's breath caught in his throat. The black tail and tawny hips of a big buckskin peaked from behind a stack of hay. He rushed forward, almost running, then he stopped. "I'm sorry," he said, looking at a big, strong, well put up buckskin. "I thought…"

"Sorry," Bob said. "Elly told me you rode a fine buckskin. We searched, but we couldn't find him. I know this isn't your horse, but he's one of the best we've ever raised, and I'd like to sell him to you."

"You raised him?"

"Sure did."

"He's a fine looking horse. Are you sure?"

"Never planned to sell him, but we've got a couple of his brothers coming along."

"I'd love to have him," Thorn said, then he pointed to a blaze faced horse. "I'll take the little sorrel too."

Bob laughed. "A redhead. Why am I not surprised? I'm just teasing. I'd have taken that one too, even if I didn't already know he was the second-best horse in the pen. He's got a deep girth, short back and long hip and he looks like he could go all day, and he can. If I was you, I'd take the blue roan too. He doesn't have the finish of the sorrel, but he's a good horse."

"What do I owe you?"

"You take them now. I'll take three bull calves in trade over the next couple of years."

"I can pay now."

"You could, but I'd rather have the bulls and you're going to need a wagon and supplies to get you through a Montana winter. Besides, I believe you're onto something, breeding more beef into our cattle. I'd like to be a part of it."

Thorn held out his hand, and they shook on it.

Elly came up from the creek with Bob and Margaret's boys Robby and Max. The boys ran to Thorn and Bob. "Look what we caught," Robby said, holding out a forked stick with four little trout on it.

"Good work men," Bob said. "Let's get inside and cook them up for breakfast." Elly strode up and placed a hand on Thorn's arm. Thorn glanced at her then looked at his boots. "I'm heading north tomorrow." Thorn said.

She squeezed his arm tighter. "You're still too weak."

"I've got to get these cattle up there and find a place and get things settled before the snow flies."

"Wait 'till spring? Bob says he could use your help until then."

"He told me that, but I've got it in me to go."

"I want you to stay."

He kicked his toe in the dirt, raising a puff of dust. "You don't know me. You don't know what I've done."

"I don't care what you've done, and I do know you. You were just a boy."

"You're too good to be saddled with someone like

me and. where I'm going, it's still wild country."

She blew out a puff of breath and let go of his arm. Tears welled in her eyes, but she turned to the house before he could see them fall.

*****

A day later Thorn, Arlin and Rufus started the cattle and the spare horses north. Thorn would pick up supplies in Cheyenne while the men kept the cattle on the trail. Bob, Margaret and the boys, waved from the porch, but Elly was nowhere to be seen. It hurt that she hadn't come to see him off, but he supposed it was better this way.

As he passed the barn, she ran out. "Wait!" she shouted.

He stopped the buckskin. "Go on boys, I'll be along."

She ran up, pulled his right hand from the saddle horn and held it in hers. She pressed something into his hand. "Find us a home," she said, her blue eyes locked on his. "Come back for me. Please. I'll wait."

Thorn looked into his hand and saw the tree-shaped pendant. He clutched it tight, "I can't take this."

"You can and you will, Thorn Marshall."

Thorn fastened the chain around his neck and tucked the pendant into his shirt. He looked into her beautiful green eyes. "You're the best woman I've ever known, Elly Strong." He pulled his hand from hers, clucked at the buckskin and started north.

The End

If you enjoyed War Wounds, the saga continues in

Family Feud. Buy it here:
https://www.amazon.com/dp/B071J8XJTZ

# Afterward

## Written November 14, 2018

Thanks! And Wow!! – not only did you read to the end of my first book, but you are reading this little afterward too.

My path to writing this book was long and winding, but it started with a love of stories. I read everything I could get my hands on. One day my Uncle Don put a Louis L'Amour novel in my hand. I'm sure I read it in one sitting. I already wanted to be a cowboy – I suppose I was one – but L'Amour taught me about the cowboy code. He showed me how strong men and women struggled and fought through hard times.

I still love throwing hay over the fence to a good saddle horse. The hardest physical job I've ever done is putting up loose hay, mowed and hauled by our team of Percheron horses, but loaded stacked and tromped into the stack by yours truly and my brave wife. If you don't believe me when I say it was T O U G H, just ask Marie. I still remember the sweet relief brought by chugging an ice-cold Pepsi while sprawled on the stack. It takes a good neighbor to know what you really need and when. Thanks Sonya! I have immense respect for the men and women who settled this land without tractors or trucks or ice-cold cola.

I've strapped on a gun and grappled with the grave responsibility, that comes with swearing an oath to serve and protect. I thank God I can only imagine the personal toll that must fall on those who kill in defending and protecting others.

I still love stories where the obstacles are insurmountable, but characters cowboy/cowgirl up and overcome. I enjoy characters who try, fail, learn, grow, and try again.

I'm a romantic. I hope each character finds love, at least for a few moments, before riding off into the sunset. Why would anyone waste all that blood, pain, and ammunition for a hot dusty ride across the desert, with only a horse and trusty pack mule for company?

So what's coming for Elly and Thorn? As you now know, Thorn had a tough life. At a young age, he lost his birth family, then he spent the war years with a rough crew. He's ready for some peace and quiet. He's ready to build something lasting. In Family Feud, despite his honest claim to only want to get to

Montana and ranch, he doesn't make it out of Cheyenne before his gunfighter self finds more trouble. Maybe he needs to learn to mind his own business. At the end of these notes, I've included a short sample of Family Feud for your enjoyment, but if you're ready to read this classic western novel, you can get it here:

FAMILY FEUD

(https://www.amazon.com/dp/B071J8XJTZ)

In book three, Cheyenne Showdown, Elly and Thorn come back together, but what should be a simple love story, turns all wrong when Thorn gets involved in Bob and Margaret's land problem.

In book four, Montana Madness, Elly decides to take matters and Thorn into her own hands, but of course, it's never that simple. If she survives, will she need, or even want, a man child, who can't make up his own mind about love?

In book five, Thorn helps his friend Oliver King and ends up badly injured. To save those he loves, King must fight the elements, the U.S. Cavalry, and his own Crow brother in law. Unfortunately, though he looks like a Montana trapper, he's a law-abiding Englishman, and he may not have what it takes.

If you are ready to read the next four books in the series, you can get the box set for a discount over individual books at: MARSHALL FAMILY WESTERN BOX SET BOOKS 2 -5 (https://www.amazon.com/dp/B07MQFZXSF/)

I wrote a short story about how Thorn ended up in the middle of the Civil War, serving Colonel Dragon Illich. I want to give you this story as a thank you gift. If you would like to find out how this kind young American boy ended up with a wild band of Red-Legged Raiders, please sign up for my newsletter at: http://www.wyattcochrane.com/

My newsletter will also alert you to my new books and other free stories, as I write and release them.

Again, thank you!

# ABOUT THE AUTHOR

Hey there, I'm Wyatt Cochrane, and once I've hung up my pistol at the end of the day and enjoyed some time roping and riding, I love to write stories. I enjoy a good tale, and I'm devoted to giving my readers fast-paced, life-or-death Western adventures. I love to throw hay over the fence to a good rope horse, and I've felt the tug on the reins when a powerful team of horses leans into their collars to start a heavy load; I've carried a gun to uphold the law, and I've grappled with the rights and wrongs of deadly force. I try to weave these feelings, sights, sounds, and smells into my stories. I love strong men and women who overcome insurmountable odds, and I always hope they find love. I enjoy hearing from readers, so please visit me at www.wyattcochrane.com

Printed in Great Britain
by Amazon

55057273R00078